Romance Unbound Publishing

Presents

Beyond the Compound

Claire Thompson

Edited by
Donna Fisk
Jae Ashley

Cover Art by Kelly Shorten
Fine Line Edit by Kathy Kozakewich

Print ISBN 978-1502369239

Chapter 1

The slave girl stood perfectly still, arms raised high over her head, crossed at the wrists. Her eyes seemed turned inward, as if she were lost inside a dream. The only hint she was suffering, indeed, that she was even aware of what was happening to her, was the slight wince that moved like a whisper of wings over her features when the whip found its mark.

The Mistress stood to the side of the slave, who faced George in all her naked splendor. Her breasts were marked with a pleasing pattern of thin red lines left behind by the perfectly aimed strokes of the whip. When the tip caught her nipple, a small sigh escaped the woman's parted lips and a tremor moved through her lithe form.

"Focus," Mistress Miriam commanded in a low, clear voice. She struck the other nipple with the knotted tip of the whip, and the slave girl's composure slipped a little more. She bit her lower lip and George could see the sheen of perspiration on her face and throat. "Remember why you exist," the Mistress intoned. "You were born for this, Hailey. Let the pain take you where you need to go."

The slave girl nodded slightly, serenity once again suffusing her delicate features. She had a narrow face, large dark blue eyes and shoulder-length blond hair, the kind that wasn't any one color, but more like a blend of pale ash, buttery yellow and shimmering gold.

"Turn," the Mistress commanded, and the woman pivoted slowly, arms still raised and crossed over her head. Christ, her ass was perfection itself — two round, lush globes absolutely made for spanking. George shifted on the sofa, using the contract he held in his hands to hide his sudden erection — not that anyone was looking at him.

The other bidder was focused squarely on the two stunning women in front of the huge stone fireplace. He didn't look much over forty, no gray yet in his slicked-back blond hair. He looked like one of those Wall Street investment banker types dressed down for the weekend, consciously casual in rumpled linen pants and Gucci loafers with no socks.

George shifted his gaze back where it belonged. The slave girl was now panting, making sexy little sounds not unlike a woman nearing orgasm, as if the whip were a cock, instead of leather, and stroking her cunt, instead of brutally marking her ass and thighs. She wasn't merely enduring this whipping with grace — she loved it. She craved it. She was perfect. He had to get her, no matter the cost.

Finally Mistress Miriam lowered the whip. "You may thank me," she said imperiously, and the girl, her entire body trembling, lowered herself as gracefully as a ballerina to the floor and pressed her pretty mouth to the toe of Mistress Miriam's shoe.

Mistress Miriam stepped back. "Kneel, at ease, facing the gentlemen," she commanded. The girl lifted herself so her back was straight. Still on her knees, she pivoted so she faced the room. She rested her hands, palms up, on her thighs, her eyes appropriately downcast, though George could see the strength in her bearing and pride in the lift of her chin.

That was all to the good. George had never favored timid, simpering women. He liked them strong and sassy—all the more fun to whip them—metaphorically and literally—into shape. At the same time, she had to be willing and eager to accept whatever devious torture her Master's active imagination and even more active libido could devise. What's more, she needed to know how to keep her mouth shut, not only during her tenure, but afterward.

George glanced down at the contract he held in his hands. Six months—the timeframe was a little long, and the starting price a little steep, but it was still within budget. The girl, of course, was disease free and also on birth control, a definite plus. Naturally he'd had to provide a clean bill of health as well. Everything else looked to be in order. No question, The Compound ran a first class operation.

George, an attorney by profession, though he no longer actively practiced, was aware this contract would never withstand the scrutiny of a court of law. It was illegal to sell one person to another, even if that person was complicit in the sale and would be handsomely paid at the end of the term. You weren't allowed to buy a sex slave and keep her under lock and key, there solely to do your sexual bidding and accept whatever erotic tortures you chose to mete out.

No matter—no courts would be involved in the process. George knew the slaves trained at The Compound received the finest education in the art of erotic submission, which included absolute obedience. In a word, Compound slaves knew to keep their mouths shut.

Another naked beauty, one of The Compound's staff slaves, glided silently into the room, carrying a bottle of the very fine Cognac she'd served them earlier in the evening. The second bidder held up his brandy snifter and the girl poured. George shook his head at the offer to replenish his glass—he was working and needed his mind clear.

Mistress Miriam sat in a chair across from George and the other bidder and crossed one long, perfect leg over the other. "As you can see," she said, "slave Hailey can take a very solid whipping with grace and courage. She is also highly sexually responsive, and extremely capable of serving a man's every sensual need and desire. Hailey craves intensity of experience. She needs a Master who will challenge her and take her to the edge of her limits and perhaps a bit beyond."

The girl remained still as a statue, a small, secret smile playing over her pretty lips. She was so young and beautiful — why would she sell herself like this to some old man she'd never met?

Money, of course. It made the world go round.

Which wasn't to say he wasn't quite impressed with what he'd seen. The tour of the facility supported the stellar reputation The Compound had garnered over the past years in the international BDSM community. Though they'd been around less than a decade, The Compound was known for producing highly trained sex slaves and placing them with carefully screened Masters around the world, and unlike some groups he'd been involved with, the slaves actually received a significant portion of the proceeds.

Maybe Mistress Miriam really did give a shit what happened to the girls she placed, but even if her motives were primarily altruistic, she was running a business. She could spout all the lofty sentiments she wanted about the art of erotic submission, and the grace and courage of their highly trained slave girls, but in the end the girl would go to the highest bidder.

"Would either of you care to examine slave Hailey before we begin the bidding?"

The other bidder rose to his feet, his eyes fixed hungrily on the naked, kneeling girl. "Yes."

Mistress Miriam turned to Hailey and lifted one eyebrow, which was apparently enough of a command to cause the girl to rise to her feet in a fluid, sensual motion that made George's bones ache with desire.

The guy strode to the front of the room. He moved with the kind of confident determination of someone used to being in charge. He stood in front of the slave girl, but George was enough off to the side that he could see what the other bidder was doing. He lifted his hand, and for a second, George thought he was going to slap the girl, but instead he gently cupped her cheek and murmured something George couldn't quite catch.

His hand slid down her cheek to her throat, his fingers gripping her just below the jawline. Hailey's pupils dilated and her lips parted. It was clear the guy was pushing some submissive buttons with his sensual chokehold.

He let her go and stepped back a little. Gripping one of her lovely nipples between forefinger and thumb, he gave it a sudden, savage twist. The girl rounded her lips into a pretty O, but otherwise made no protest. The guy slapped at her thigh and she widened her stance, bare feet flat on the stone hearth.

Again he murmured something George couldn't quite catch. The girl tilted her pelvis forward, her face outwardly serene, though George couldn't help but wonder what was going on in that pretty head of hers.

The man gripped her vulva like he was grabbing a piece of fruit. He must have been doing something with his fingers, judging by the pretty pink blush that moved over Hailey's throat and cheeks and the way her head fell slightly back. "Oh," she breathed, the word like fingers stroking George's cock. This one would be a prize, no question about it.

The second bidder withdrew his hand and nudged the girl's shoulder. She pirouetted so her back was to them, and George fondled that perfect ass with his eyes, even as the man used his hands to do the same thing. Finally the man returned to his seat.

Mistress Miriam turned to George. "And you, Sir?"

George shook his head. He'd seen all he needed to know. The girl was perfect. He cleared his throat. "I'm good, thanks."

"Slave Hailey," Mistress Miriam said, "you may wait in my office."

"Yes, Mistress," the girl said softly. Her voice was low and throaty, and George wondered how she'd sound in the throes of orgasm.

Once the girl was gone, Mistress Miriam faced the two men. "As we've previously discussed the contract has a six-month tenure, with a renewal clause at the end of the term. The initial bid is two hundred thousand dollars, half to be paid up front to The Compound, the other half to be maintained in an account for the slave until the end of her term of service. As you know, we don't generally have bidding for our contracts, instead usually matching a particular Master with a particular slave for an agreed upon price. But since you both seem intent on procuring this particular slave, I've decided this is the most equitable solution to the issue."

And the most profitable for you, George thought, though of course he didn't say this aloud.

"Two fifty," the other bidder promptly said.

"Two sixty," George rejoined.

"Two seventy."

"Two eighty."

The other bidder was silent for several beats, and George imagined he was calculating how much of a bonus his bank would give him that year, and if Hailey was worth the price. The guy brought his hand to his face, the hand that had been buried in the beauty's cunt a moment before and closed his eyes, as if inhaling her sensual perfume. Apparently it was enough to push him to the next step.

"Three hundred," he said, casting a triumphant look in George's direction, as if to say, *top that, old man.*

You bet your ass I will, George silently responded. The guy had no clue who he was up against. Time to end this thing.

"Three fifty," George said softly, his eyes fixed on Mistress Miriam.

Silence for several beats. George kept his eyes on Mistress Miriam, each passing second a small triumph. *Going once, going twice...*

"If that's the final bid..." Mistress Miriam said, letting the sentence trail away.

George finally permitted himself to glance at his competition. The guy pressed his lips into a thin line and George could see the struggle on his face. He wanted the girl, but the price was too steep. Finally he gave a small, sharp shake of his head.

Victory!

Mistress Miriam stood and extended her hand to George, who stood as well, trying to keep the goofy grin from his face. "Slave Hailey is one of the most highly trained and deeply submissive slaves The Compound has ever produced," she said as she gripped his hand with her long, cool fingers. "I think you will be very happy."

Yeah. I'd be delirious with joy, George thought wryly, *if only she were for me.*

~*~

Hailey cast a sideways glance at the man sitting beside her as they winged their way across the country in the first private jet Hailey had ever been in. He was a good-looking guy for his age, which she guessed was somewhere in the mid fifties. He had a thick head of silver hair, clear blue eyes, a still firm jaw and craggy features. But if she were honest, she had to admit she'd been rooting for the younger Master.

No point in wasting time on what might have been, so she put the thought out of her head. She would focus instead on doing the best she could for the man who had chosen her. Age not withstanding, Master George seemed honest, kind, and serious about the lifestyle, all of which were excellent points in his favor.

After two months of intensive training at The Compound, and a lifetime of searching for, and as yet never finding, a true Master who would make her his own, Hailey had given herself over to the process. Though she recognized the artificiality inherent in placing herself under contract to a virtual stranger, at the same time she trusted Mistress Miriam to place her with someone of integrity and quality.

She needed a Master who would intuitively understand and respect her deep-seated longing to submit—body and soul—to another person. She needed someone as dedicated and committed to the lifestyle as she was. In hindsight, it was evident in the past she'd made a mistake in seeking a lover who was dominant, rather than a Dominant who might in time become a lover. True that wasn't likely to happen with this man who was old enough to be her father, but that was okay. She would learn and grow from the experience, and hopefully make him happy and proud to own her for the duration of the contract. After that—who knew?

Energized by her internal pep talk, Hailey decided to begin their new relationship by telling Master George she was honored to have this opportunity to serve him, and would make every effort to give him the best of her submission.

"Permission to speak, Sir?" Hailey ventured.

The man turned to her, as if surprised by the question. "You don't need permission. Not with me."

Had she heard him correctly? "I'm sorry, I don't understand, Sir."

He smiled. "Listen. Now that everything's wrapped up and we're on our way to your new life for the next six months, I need to level with you, Hailey."

A sliver of unease sliced its way through Hailey's gut. Surely the time to level, whatever that meant, had come before they were headed across the country, where she'd promised to serve as his personal sex slave for the next six months? Hailey willed herself to remain calm. Slaves were patient. Slaves didn't anticipate—they accepted. She waited, her eyes fixed on Master George's face.

He blew out a breath, as if steeling himself for what he had to say. "I'm afraid I've procured you under false pretenses."

"False pretenses?" Hailey echoed, thoroughly confused and unsettled by this admission.

"Mistress Miriam was aware of the arrangements," George continued, "but I didn't mention them to you until now because discretion is of the utmost importance to my client. I did buy your contract, or rather, I negotiated its purchase, but I'm not the one who will own you for the next six months."

Hailey realized she was clutching the armrests of her seat with a white-knuckled grip. Willing herself to relax, she moved her hands into her lap and folded them together while her mind struggled to process what the man was saying.

"The person who bought you doesn't like to make himself a target for the public. He's a very private man in his personal life. That's why he couldn't come himself, much as he would have liked to. I'm his personal representative in certain transactions. He's—well, you'll see when you meet him."

Even while Hailey's mind was trying to let go of the idea that this kind, older man would *not* be her Master for the next six months, she was deeply intrigued by what he was saying. Who was this mystery man she was being delivered to?

Someone famous. It had to be. But why not just tell her? And even if the guy was some kind of celebrity or big shot, why go to such lengths? It wasn't like anyone at The Compound would care who the guy was, surely? They were part of a BDSM community that understood the need for discretion. Folks seriously committed to the lifestyle were well aware of the discrimination, intolerance and basic misunderstanding that existed out there.

Unless—oh shit—what if the man she signed her life away to for the next half year was one of those fanatical, pseudo-religious types? Someone who couldn't risk showing his face in a so-called den of iniquity? One of those smarmy creeps who amassed a fortune by preaching against sinners like homosexuals and other deviants, and then were caught with their pants around their ankles, their cocks down another guy's throat? Someone who would spend the next six months forcing Hailey to atone for her "sins"?

What the hell have I done?

The sliver of unease bloomed into a fist of panic that clutched at Hailey's gut. She closed her eyes and drew in and then released a deep, cleansing breath. She called on all her grace and submission training, bringing it around her like a warm, comforting cloak. *Stay calm. Don't jump to conclusions. Mistress Miriam would never place you with someone like that. Whatever happens, submit with grace and courage. Accept what is offered, and serve with passion.*

"Hey," Master George, or was he just George, said gently, placing a hand on her shoulder. "You okay? You're looking a little pale. Are you motion sick?"

Hailey opened her eyes and forced a smile. "No, thank you. I'm okay. Just still not really clear on what you're telling me. I'm trying to adjust to this change in plans. I thought you were the one who bought me."

A spasm of pain seemed to move over the man's face. "Don't I wish," he said in an undertone so that she barely caught the words.

She had to know what was going on, and so she pressed, "Do I know this person you're taking me to? Can you tell me his name?"

George seemed to ponder the question. "Okay, you're right," he finally said. "You deserve to know, and anyway, you'll know soon enough. It's Ronan Wolfe. That's who bought you."

Hailey struggled to place the name. An actor. That was it. He was in the movies. Which explained why they were headed out to California. Yes, he must be an actor, though for the life of her, she couldn't conjure a face to go with the name.

At twenty-eight, Hailey knew she was definitely in the minority in her generation. A yoga teacher by profession, she didn't own a computer or a television. Her cell phone wasn't smart at all. She rarely went to the movies, and in fact couldn't remember the last time she'd been to one. She vastly preferred to lose herself in a good book, or in peaceful meditation beside the creek at the back of her cottage in her small Vermont town.

George was regarding her expectantly, and so she said, "He's an actor, right?"

His expression went from confusion to incredulity to amusement within the space of a few seconds. He burst out laughing, a big guffaw that made her smile back in spite of herself. "Good one. You had me going for a second there."

Hailey was confused. "You mean he's not an actor?"

George tilted his head, his eyebrows lifted in disbelief. "You mean you honestly don't know who Ronan Wolfe is? The biggest heartthrob of the decade? The man who's been described as Gregory Peck, Paul Newman and George Clooney all rolled into one incredible package of artistic talent and devastating good looks?"

"I'm sorry," Hailey replied lamely. "I don't go to the movies much."

"I guess not. Or watch TV. Or live in the modern world." His tone dripped with sarcasm and Hailey felt herself coloring. She looked away so he wouldn't see her blush.

"I'm sorry." George's tone had changed to one of contrition. She felt his hand again on her arm. "That was uncalled for." George gave a small laugh. "I should be impressed to be with the one straight woman in America who doesn't fall into a dead faint at the prospect of meeting Ronan Wolfe in the flesh."

Hailey offered an apologetic shrug, not sure what to say. If this guy was as famous as all that, she would surely recognize him when she saw him, she supposed. The prospect of serving a man who probably had an ego the size of Montana wasn't exactly thrilling, but he was clearly serious about owning a trained submissive, given all the trouble he'd gone to in order to procure her.

Unless... Unless he just had more money than he knew what to do with, and had jumped on the BDSM bandwagon as something kinky and fun to try out? Was she being consigned to spend six months with a dabbler in the scene? A vapid, clueless celebrity looking to explore a casual kink?

True, the money was great—she would pocket more from this six-month contract than she earned in five years as a yoga instructor—but money hadn't been her primary motivator when she signed on for training at The Compound. She was seeking a true connection with a bona fide BDSM Master. The idea of being a casual play toy for some wannabe Dom was not appealing, even if he was god's gift to women.

"Is he serious about the lifestyle?" she ventured. "I mean," she added hastily, "I don't mean any disrespect, but is Mr. Wolfe just, um, you know, just doing this for fun? Has he done anything like this before?"

"You can rest easy on that score, Hailey. I've known Ronan for a long time, and he's no lightweight looking for a bit of slap and tickle. He's heavily into the scene, and though I'm not sure he's looking for love"—George offered a wry smile as he said this—"he's as serious as you are about BDSM."

Hailey let out a breath she hadn't realized she'd been holding. "The thing is," George continued, "because of who he is, and the work he does, he can't really afford to have it out there that he's into the lifestyle. The press would have a field day if they found out the guy was into whips and chains, which is how they would characterize it. Ronan's a very private guy, and he doesn't want his private business to become fodder for the gossip mills. I'm sure you heard about his big breakup with Jennifer St. Claire and that whole mess a few years back."

Hailey opened her mouth to say yes, of course, as she desperately tried to summon up who Jennifer St. Claire might be, and George laughed again. "Oh, right," he said, still chuckling. "I forgot. I'm dealing with the one woman in the country who doesn't give a shit about Hollywood royalty." He patted her knee. "Anyway, the press had a real field day with that one, and most of what they reported had zero basis in fact, but they didn't let that bother them, of course. Can you imagine what they'd do if they found out Ronan had a live-in, trained slave girl?"

Hailey could only imagine. She didn't particularly relish the idea of being splashed across the tabloids either. Though she wasn't ashamed of her submissive leanings or lifestyle, she did live in the real world, too, and had no desire to be embroiled in any kind of scandal.

They were quiet for a while, and Hailey was glad for the silence as she tried to collect her thoughts and feelings. Master George was just George—a procurer for this famous but reclusive celebrity who was seeking a sub girl, but not love.

Okay, fine. It was better to be prepared in advance for what she was getting into, and though she would have appreciated knowing these facts before she'd signed on the dotted line, would her decision have been any different if she'd known the truth?

Her first and best yoga and meditation instructor, Deirdre Levy, used to say something to Hailey when she experienced a setback in her progress or hit a roadblock of some kind. "Remember, dear heart," her mentor would tell her with a kind smile, "everything happens for a reason and a purpose, and it serves you."

Hailey had never entirely bought the concept that everything happened for a particular reason—there was definitely bad, random shit out there in the universe that could smack you in the face and hurl you to the ground. This was brutally confirmed in Hailey's mind when Deirdre died later that year of ovarian cancer at the absurdly young age of forty-two.

But she did like the concept of taking those random events, both good and bad, and figuring out how they could serve her. Whatever happened in California, it was up to Hailey to make it work. Not to make the best of it in the sense of submitting to a fate beyond one's control, but rather to learn from whatever happened, to grow from it and take something good from it.

Finding out about The Compound from a dear friend in the scene, and then getting accepted for the training, had been both the best and most challenging experience of Hailey's life.

Until now.

Somehow she had a feeling these next six months would prove even more of a challenge. But she would make it serve her. She would rise to the occasion. She would serve Master Ronan with all the passion and courage she possessed. And she would put that lingering thought of finding true love aside for now.

The flight attendant, a pleasant young man named Carlo, appeared carrying a tray loaded with fresh fruit, various cheeses, bread and crackers, plus two bottles of Perrier water, all of which he set on the table between their large, comfortable seats. "Some light refreshment for you," he said with a professional smile. "We should be arriving in about two hours."

He picked up the bottle of champagne that he'd left chilling in a bucket of ice on a side bar. "Would you care for some champagne?"

"I most certainly would," George said enthusiastically. He turned to Hailey. "How about you?"

"I would love some."

Carlo popped the cork and poured the sparkling wine into two crystal flutes. "Do let me know if there's anything else," he said, and then disappeared.

George lifted his hand in a toast, and Hailey clinked the edge of her glass to his. "To youth and money," he said with a wink. "If I had either, I would make you my own." He laughed, another big guffaw, and then downed his glass in one gulp.

Chapter 2

We're here.

Ronan read the words on his cell screen and a few seconds later heard the sound of the gates at the front of the property whirring slowly open. He pushed himself to his feet and headed inside from the back deck, his eyes taking a second to adjust to the dim light. He moved quickly through the large house to the front room.

From the window he watched George's car pull to a stop. A sense of the surreal settled over him. Was this really happening? Not for the first time, he began to question himself and this whole crazy arrangement. Was he out of his fucking mind to have let George convince him to do this thing? Had he really just *bought* another human being to use for his sexual and sadistic pleasure?

As George hoisted two large suitcases from the trunk, the passenger door opened and the girl Ronan had just spent a fortune to procure slid gracefully out of the car. He held his breath, his heart skipping a beat.

She had silky blond hair that Ronan's practiced eye detected was natural. She wore a dark blue sundress with spaghetti straps. Her limbs were long, with smooth, well-defined muscle beneath lightly tanned skin. Her legs were bare, her feet shod in simple, flat sandals. She moved with the easy, lanky grace of an athlete.

"Here goes nothing," he murmured, reaching for the door. He pulled it open, mentally preparing for the usual wide-eyed expression of excitement and adoration with which all women and not a few men characteristically greeted him, and which always made him vaguely uncomfortable. He wasn't so stupid as to believe any of the gushing sentiment routinely spewed in his direction was for Ronan Wolfe, the man. What they admired or envied had little to do with him as a person. It was just part of the whole glitzy package, the brand that was heavily marketed as *Ronan Wolfe, movie star heartthrob.*

To his surprise, Hailey's large, dark blue eyes moved over his face without a flicker of emotion, save for a shy smile, before she looked demurely down. She stood stock-still, waiting, he realized, for him to do or say something. George stood just behind the girl, suitcases in either hand, a big smile on his face.

"Well, don't just stand there," his best friend said with a laugh. "Help out an old man. Take these things before I drop them."

"Oh, sorry." Ronan stepped forward to take the suitcases from George as Hailey stepped nimbly to the side. As she moved, their arms brushed, skin on skin, and he caught the faint scent of her perfume — something spicy and warm.

As George handed over her suitcases, he chuckled. "Not that she'll be needing much of what's in there. You like your slave girls naked, isn't that right, Master Ronan?" He snorted. "You lucky bastard."

Ronan glanced at the girl. She kept her eyes down, though he thought he detected the faint creep of a blush along her cheeks.

He realized he was staring. "Come inside, please," Ronan said, finally remembering his manners. Suitcases in tow, he stepped back into the front hall, gesturing with his chin for them to enter.

George reached into his jacket and pulled out a large envelope, which he held out to Ronan. "Here's the contract—signed, sealed and delivered. This delicious morsel of a girl is all yours for the next six months. Don't fuck it up, Ronan. She's the real deal. A bona fide submissive, trained by the finest in the business. Even better, she hasn't a fucking clue who you are. How do you like them apples?"

"What?" Ronan said, disbelief making the word pop out of his mouth.

"Yeah," George said, eyebrows raised. "Hard to believe right? There's a person left in this country, hell, in the world, who isn't aware that Ronan Wolfe has been voted the sexiest man alive by the rabid fans who read *People Magazine* for the last three years running. Crazy, right?" His sarcastic tone was offset by his lopsided grin and kind, crinkling eyes. Ronan realized how few people there were left in his world who didn't try to "handle" him, and the realization left him at once grateful for George, and lonely as hell.

Ronan stared down at the envelope in his hands and then back up at George, still not quite ready to come to grips with what he had signed up for. "Want to come inside and have a quick beer?" he said. He glanced at Hailey, wondering if he should offer her one too.

George shook his head and took a step back. "Sorry, I can't stay. I've got to see a guy about a thing." He offered an exaggerated wink. "She's all yours, my friend. Use her in good health." Turning to Hailey, he added enigmatically, "Youth and money, babe. Makes the world go 'round."

George returned to his car, climbed in and started the engine. He rolled down the window and waved as he drove away down the long driveway, leaving the two of them alone.

Hailey stood silently, her arms hanging loosely at her sides, her posture ramrod straight, her eyes downcast. "Come inside," Ronan said, gesturing her into the front hall. He closed the door and then slipped a finger under the seal of the envelope George had given him. Lifting the flap, he pulled out the contract and scanned it.

I promise to serve and obey my Master to the very best of my ability for the tenure of this contract. I freely give my body, my obedience, my service and my trust to my Master in exchange for his guidance and loving dominance. Save for the hard limits listed below, my Master may press the envelope of my submission as far as he deems appropriate, and I will submit with grace and honesty to his will.

He scanned down to the hard limits section and read: *No scat, no animals, no minors.*

That sure left room for a whole lot of dark and dirty play, and the sadistic devil that was always perched on Ronan's shoulder, whether or not there was a balancing angel present, rubbed its hot little hands together as his overactive libido shifted into overdrive.

He looked again at the sub girl who stood still as a living statue, no fidgeting or toe tapping, or any sign of anxiety on her serene face, though she had to be going nuts on the inside. Maybe the full import of what she'd done was sinking in for her too, or maybe she was in it solely for the money, and really didn't give a damn what she had to do in order to get it. After all, he'd paid a small fortune for her services and was aware she stood to pocket half the proceeds at the end of her tenure with him.

Even as this snarky thought flitted into Ronan's brain, his better self dismissed it. George was an unerring judge of character, and he'd vouched for Hailey. Even without George's assistance, Ronan could see for himself there was something genuine in this girl. It was evident in the videos he'd watched of her training sessions at The Compound, and he had felt it just now in her somber, sweet gaze. Whatever else she might be, she was sincere in her desire for erotic submission.

Used to the glamor and glitz of LA, it was startling to realize she didn't appear to be wearing any makeup or jewelry. He could see the perk of her nipples against the silky fabric of her short dress.

Christ, she was lovely. And she was *his*. Who the hell had ever said money couldn't buy happiness? He was staring at a hundred and ten pounds of pure feminine perfection, with no strings, no expectations, no limits. What was he waiting for?

Let's get this party started.

"Take off your sandals," he said.

She slipped off her shoes and stepped neatly to the side.

"Take off your dress."

Eyes still demurely downcast, Hailey reached for one strap and slid it down her shoulder. He watched, mesmerized, as she reached for the other, and let the dress slither down her shapely body and puddle at her feet. Underneath she wore nothing but a tiny white lace thong. Though Ronan had seen plenty of naked women, this girl could hold her own among the finest of them, with her high, round breasts, tapering waist and gently flaring hips. His mouth actually watered at the sight of her, and he had to swallow to keep from choking. His rapidly rising cock was bent at a painful angle in his jeans, and he reached into his pants to straighten it.

He stepped closer. She remained where she was. He put a finger underneath her chin and lifted it. She met his gaze, her pupils dilating, her breath catching ever so slightly as her lips parted. Her scent was like an aphrodisiac, and he felt almost dizzy from it.

"Who do you belong to?" he said, lust making his voice come out as a growl.

"To you, Master Ronan." Her voice was like fingertips on satin, stroking his senses.

Ronan's cock hardened to steel. He *owned* this girl, and she wasn't just some high-class call girl he'd bought for the night. She was fully trained in the sensual and submissive arts. She was his personal geisha girl, only better. She was his willing slave girl, and he could do whatever he wanted, with no one to judge, witness, oversee or deny him. For the first time in his life, he could give free rein to his kinkiest fantasies, without fear his exploits would end up in tomorrow's tabloid headlines, and without worry about what the girl thought or felt about it all. After all, she was his possession, not his lover. The same rules did not apply. In fact, beyond keeping her alive and safe from harm, there *were* no rules, save that she please him or suffer the consequences.

As the full import of this finally hit him, Ronan took a step back and pointed at his fly. "Show me," he ordered. "Show me what you can do. You may use your mouth and your hands."

Without hesitation, the girl dropped to her knees, her long, slender fingers reaching for the metal button at the top of his fly. She slid down the zipper and hooked her thumbs over the waist of his jeans and underwear. She pulled the pants down his legs to his knees and wrapped long, cool fingers around the base of his shaft, her other hand gently cupping his balls as she leaned forward with parted lips.

She took the full length of him into her mouth, moving forward until her nose touched his groin. She remained like that for several delicious moments, Ronan's cock pulsing against her wet, soft tongue and the hug of her throat. As she eased back, she did something amazing with her throat muscles and tongue, and in spite of himself Ronan groaned aloud.

Maybe because it had been a while since he'd been with a woman (tabloid rumors and outright lies to the contrary notwithstanding), or maybe because of the novelty of the situation, or maybe because she was just so damn good at what she was doing, it wasn't long before Ronan was ready to spurt.

Instinctively he reached for her head, grabbing handfuls of silky hair between his fingers as he thrust his hips forward in sudden, urgent release. He held her in position until the last of his seed had spilled down her throat, and she neither moved nor resisted. She wasn't even breathing, as far as he could tell. Finally he let her go and took a step back. She let his still-hard cock slide from her pretty lips.

Her hair had fallen into her eyes, but she made no effort to shake or move it away. Her face was flushed, her lips wet and parted, her nipples perking like dark pink gumdrops.

"Thank you, Sir." She bent forward, lowering her body until her lips met the tops of his bare feet. She brushed one foot and then the other with her soft lips and then lifted herself back onto her haunches, her spine straightening again into dancer-like perfection as her hands settled gracefully on her thighs.

Ronan pulled up his underwear and jeans as he stared down at the sub girl. "You're welcome," he finally managed, marveling even as he spoke at the understatement of his words. Jesus god, the girl was perfection, and they hadn't even made it out of the front hall.

~*~

His eyes were a striking shade of luminous green, the color of sea glass. They were further set off by glossy, dark hair that kept falling rakishly into his face. He exuded a kind of raw but contained sexual power of which he seemed completely unaware. His features were strong, his jaw firm, his bearing and physique the stuff of romance novel covers. Though Hailey had never thought of herself as someone hung up on physical appearances, there was something about this guy that made it hard to look away.

Since the moment she'd seen him, Hailey kept having to remind herself a properly trained slave didn't stare boldly into her Master's face. She should have been prepared for a handsome guy, based on George's assertion of his fame, but normally somewhat indifferent to outward appearances, she hadn't expected her own strong reaction to his masculine beauty. Even if the guy had zero talent, he was what some of her younger yoga students referred to as serious eye candy.

She took his offered hand and allowed him to pull her upright.

He dropped her hand. "You thirsty?"

"Yes, Sir," she replied, the question suddenly reminding her she was parched.

He led her through a cathedral-ceiling living room, which contained dark wood furniture covered in spotless white upholstery. One entire wall of the large room was made of glass, with a breathtaking view of the Pacific Ocean just beyond the floor to ceiling windows.

She walked behind him, admiring his easy, powerful grace as he moved. He was wearing jeans and a short-sleeved white shirt that fit loosely over broad shoulders and the hint of a muscular back. She liked that he was barefoot. She herself only wore shoes when absolutely necessary.

He turned toward her as he moved through a large archway and gestured for her to precede him into a spacious kitchen with stainless steel appliances, granite countertops and a stone-tiled floor. "Would you like a beer? Or there's some fresh limeade in the fridge."

"Limeade, please, Sir." She felt dizzy enough without the addition of liquor, though she kept this to herself. She could still taste the faint mushroomy flavor of his semen in the back of her throat. Fellatio hadn't been her strong suit when she'd arrived at The Compound, and her trainers had spent a lot of time working with her on technique. Hopefully she'd satisfied her new Master.

Though she found Ronan Wolfe very pleasing to the eye, she hadn't been expecting the sharp, visceral thrill that had shot through her body when she'd closed her mouth over his thick, satiny cock and inhaled the spicy sweetness of his musk. She'd been so focused these last months on learning to be a properly trained submissive and making herself worthy to be someone's sex slave, that she'd somehow forgotten her own desires in the process. That impromptu session in the foyer had reignited them with a whoosh, like gasoline thrown onto dying flames.

She watched as Ronan took out a large glass pitcher of juice and set it on the counter. He pulled two glasses from the cabinet. "May I serve you, Sir?" she asked.

He turned toward her with raised eyebrows. "You just did that, no?"

She looked down, suddenly afraid she'd overstepped. She needed to know the house rules.

Possibly she had spoken out of turn. "I'm sorry, Sir. I meant—"

He cut her off with a laugh. "Hey, I'm just being a jerk. You want to serve the juice?" He shrugged and leaned against the large island in the center of the room. "Sure. Go ahead. There's ice if you want it." He pointed toward the refrigerator. "I like mine without."

She did too. She lifted the pitcher and poured the limeade. She handed one of the glasses to Ronan and waited for him to drink before lifting her glass to her lips. She drank deeply of the fresh, tangy juice, feeling it revive her as it went down. When she finished, she realized Ronan was staring at her, his glass barely touched, his lips quirked in an amused smile. "Thirsty, huh?"

She felt the warmth move over her cheeks. "Yes, Sir," she said.

"Want some more?" He gestured toward the pitcher.

Hailey realized she needed to pee. "No, thank you, Sir." She started to ask for permission to use the bathroom, but Ronan was speaking, and so she closed her mouth.

"Okay, then. Let me show you around, and go over some of the ground rules for your stay here."

"Yes, Sir."

They returned to the foyer. Ronan gestured toward her dress and sandals. "Grab that stuff, will you?" As Hailey retrieved her things, Ronan picked up her suitcases. "Whatever you have in here, you won't be needing, at least not the clothing. We're in sunny California and I have complete privacy here on my property. And George was right. I do like my slave girls naked."

Slave girls.

How many had he owned before her? Where were they now?

She followed Ronan again through the huge living room. This time he led her to the wide, curving staircase at the back of the room. Once at the top, she expected him to go down the wide hallway, but instead Ronan turned toward a door set into the back wall and pulled it open. "This way," he said, starting up a smaller set of rather steep stairs.

The stairs opened onto a large windowless room. Ronan flicked on the lights and revealed a fully equipped BDSM dungeon, complete with a cross, a spanking bench, a leather swing and two cages, one upright, the other long and low. There was a wooden apparatus that looked quite diabolical. It had a roller at the top and a fixed bar at the bottom, with leather cuffs dangling from chains at various intervals.

The dungeon floor was covered with soft, thick carpeting. One wall held a wide array of whips and floggers hanging on hooks, along with coils of rope and chain. A high counter set against the wall was lined with cuffs, clips, clamps, blindfolds and enough BDSM paraphernalia to stock a small store.

Hailey took it all in with shining eyes, her cunt and nipples gently throbbing with desire. Her skin ached with the need to feel the snug grip of tight rope and the sensual burn of leather. She turned to Master Ronan, who was regarding her intently, his smile lurking just beneath the surface, like a shark in shallow water.

"Like what you see, slave girl?" he murmured. Dropping the suitcases, he moved behind her and wrapped his arms around her. Though she'd been whipped, penetrated, bound and brought to orgasm time and again at The Compound, one thing she hadn't been was held. She was, she realized suddenly, bereft of touch. Unable to resist the siren's call of his unexpected embrace, she leaned into him, her body molding perfectly against his.

"Oh, yes, Sir," she breathed.

"Good. You'll be spending most of your time here."

His arms fell away. It took every ounce of control for Hailey not to turn toward him and grab him. She wanted to bury her face in his chest and beg him to hold her—just hold her. Instead she took a deep breath and forced herself to recall her training. She was not this man's lover. She was his purchased slave, and her duty was to serve, not to demand.

Obviously unaware of her inner turmoil, Ronan retrieved the suitcases. "Let me show you where you'll be sleeping," he said, gesturing with his head for her to follow. He walked through the room toward an open door at the back of the dungeon. He passed through the doorway, Hailey following behind.

This room wasn't much bigger than a large closet, though a skylight in the ceiling saved it from feeling claustrophobic. The room contained a bureau and a mattress on the floor. A tiny lamp was set directly in an outlet on the wall beside the mattress. The mattress was covered in a clean white sheet, a single pillow at the head of the bed, a pale blue coverlet folded at the foot. A long sturdy chain lay coiled in the center of the mattress, one end of it rising along the wall, where it was affixed to a thick metal eyebolt.

Through another doorway, Hailey could see tiled flooring and a sink. Following her gaze, Ronan said, "That's your bathroom. This is the slave quarters. You will sleep here when I'm not using you." The words sent an involuntary shudder though Hailey's frame. The training was over. The dream had become a reality. It was happening. This was real.

Master Ronan set down the cases. "Unpack and put away your things. You may use the bathroom, shower, whatever you need to do." He moved toward the bureau and opened the top drawer. He reached in and turned toward her with something in his hands.

He held up a slim black leather collar with O-rings set at intervals around its perimeter. Hailey's hand went reflexively to her neck. She'd worn the standard issue red canvas training collar while at The Compound, but it had been removed when she'd completed her training. The skin on her bare neck actually tingled in anticipation of wearing Master Ronan's collar.

"You will wear this collar at all times during your stay here, except while showering." He pointed to the floor and Hailey sank to her knees, bowing her head forward in offering. She nearly sighed aloud with pleasure as the welcoming leather was secured around her throat and buckled into place. When Master Ronan was done, she rose again to her feet, lifting her chin so he could see his handiwork.

He nodded, his luminous green eyes glittering. "Take off the panties. You will not wear underwear again for the duration of your stay."

Hailey immediately slipped off the bit of silk and lace covering her smooth mons and kept her gaze lowered as she felt Ronan's eyes moving over her form. She wasn't shy of her body, made lean and strong by years of yoga, but she also knew this man could have his pick of any woman he chose. By some miraculous quirk of fate, he'd chosen her.

At least for a while.

"Hands behind your head," he snapped suddenly, and Hailey hastened to obey. "Spread your legs and tilt your pelvis forward." His voice had deepened, the authority ringing in his tone. Hailey did as she was ordered, her heart quickening against her ribs.

He moved closer. She could feel his breath on her cheek as he reached down between her legs. He cupped her mons and slipped one thick, hard finger inside her, the suddenness of his movement making her gasp, even as her cunt sucked down on the digit. After a steady diet of constant sexual stimulation, Hailey hadn't been permitted an orgasm during the last week of her training, and her body was now quivering with need. It took all her focus to keep from wantonly bucking against her new Master's hand.

Master Ronan chuckled, the sound low and sensual. "You're soaking wet," he announced. "I like that. If I ever find you dry, slave, I will punish you."

"Yes, Sir," Hailey whispered faintly, her nipples aching.

"By the same token," he continued, as he slipped a second finger in beside the first, "your body belongs to me. If I ever find you touching yourself without my express direction, or orgasming without my command, you will be whipped until I draw blood. Are we quite clear on this, slave?"

"Yes, Sir," Hailey breathed, the muscles of her cunt spasming against his fingers, which he was moving sensually inside her. If he didn't stop soon, she was going to be in serious trouble.

As suddenly as he'd penetrated her, he withdrew his fingers. He brought them to his nose and inhaled, his eyes fluttering closed for a moment, a small smile whispering across his face.

Dropping his hand, he opened his eyes. "Come here," he said in a low, urgent voice. He opened his arms, and Hailey moved into them. He gathered her close and leaned down, dipping his head until their lips touched. Hailey sighed against his mouth as he kissed her. Her lips parted as his tongue slipped past them. She felt herself melting against him, and she would have fallen to the floor if he hadn't been holding her so tightly.

He kissed her for a long time, his hands roaming her back and cupping her ass as he explored her mouth with his. When he finally let her go, she felt the loss of him so keenly, it was as if all the air had been sucked from her lungs. She gasped in her struggle to recover her equilibrium.

Ronan seemed to be enduring some kind of internal struggle of his own. It was as if a shade had been drawn over his brilliant green eyes, his expression difficult to read.

"I'll return in twenty minutes," he finally said, the urgency that had been in his tone a moment before now replaced with a cool authority. Had she only imagined the passion in his kiss? Or was she the only one who had felt it?

"I expect to find you standing at attention in the dungeon, hands locked behind your head," he continued. "I've seen what you're capable of in the videos, but I've always liked to check things out for myself. I want to see how you handle various sorts of erotic pain and sensual restraint. I'm going to test your limits, Hailey. The Compound was the audition, but now you've got the part. It's showtime, and I expect you to give me all you've got."

Whatever had just happened — or not happened — a moment before, his words recalled her to her duty, thrilling her with their promise. Hailey sank once more to her knees and showered the tops of his bare feet with tiny kisses. While a part of her was terrified that she might fail this new stern Master, she knew in her bones she had found her place at last. This was what she had wanted — what she had dreamed of.

He tapped her shoulder and she rose once more to her feet, watching as he left the small room and strode toward the dungeon stairs. She touched the collar and offered a silent prayer to the BDSM gods.

Please, don't let me fuck this up.

Chapter 3

Ronan stepped into the attic dungeon and stopped just inside the door to drink in the sight. The slave girl stood perfectly still, hands behind her head, her dark blue eyes open but gazing at some distant point beyond the confines of the space.

He had changed out of his clothes before returning to the dungeon, and wore only a pair of white shorts. The air in the attic dungeon was warm, despite the pleasant spring day outside. Hailey's hair was damp, her skin slightly pink, presumably from a quick shower, or was she sweating? He flicked on the switch that activated the two huge ventilation fans set high on either side of the room and a cool breeze flowed through the space.

His eyes moved lovingly over all the sexy equipment he'd amassed over the past year in anticipation of this moment. The realization he would soon christen the devices using the slave girl standing before him sent a mule kick of adrenaline to his chest.

She gave no sign she had heard him enter. She stood at attention, her breasts thrust proudly forward, chin raised, legs precisely shoulder-width apart. How long could she stand there without moving? That in itself might be an interesting test, especially if he threw some predicament bondage into the mix.

Ronan touched his lips as he regarded Hailey. He hadn't meant to kiss her. Hopefully she hadn't gotten the wrong idea from that kiss. They were, most emphatically, not lovers. He had purchased her. She was property. If he wanted to kiss his property, that was his right. Still, he would need to be careful. Women, even highly trained sexual submissives, were apt to get the wrong idea if you got too lovey dovey.

Ronan glanced around the dungeon, wondering where to begin. All the training and practice in the domination arts he'd put in over the past year at The Exchange Club would finally be brought to bear. She wasn't the only one moving from the audition phase to the real thing.

He entered the room and came to a stop directly in front of Hailey, purposely invading her personal space. She didn't even blink. He cupped her breasts and lifted them, loving the sweet heft and soft give of them, delighted she hadn't decided to augment them into melon-hard, gravity-defying beach balls, as so many women in Hollywood seemed compelled to do. He reached for her nipples, rolling them until they stiffened. He pinched them and twisted.

Her only reaction was a slight flaring of the nostrils.

"A few rules," he said, his fingers still tight on her nipples. "You will not speak without express permission, except to answer direct questions. The exception to this, of course, is if you're in distress and I don't seem to be getting it, though a safeword should suffice in that instance. You will answer all questions promptly, and with complete honesty, even if it's something you don't think I want to hear. Understood?"

"Yes, Sir," Hailey managed as he twisted again. She winced, but her nipples had hardened to points. He twisted harder and then let go suddenly, reaching for her throat with his left hand, his fingers finding and digging into the soft flesh just below her jaw. As he squeezed, he slapped her cheek with his right hand, the smacking sound of his palm cracking in the air.

Hailey's eyes widened, her face reddening from his tight grip around her throat. "Ah, so you're not a statue," Ronan said, his cock tenting his shorts. He let go of her throat, and as she gasped for a breath, he slapped her again.

Without giving her a chance to recover, he demanded, "What's your safeword?"

"Bubblegum, Sir," she said in a breathless voice.

"Bubblegum," Ronan repeated, amused at the odd choice.

He stepped back, rubbing his chin as he thought about what he might try next. "You know, I've seen the videos of you being flogged and whipped, and you're quite impressive in your ability to withstand erotic pain."

"Thank you, Sir," Hailey replied softly. Her chest was rising and falling as she struggled to regain her composure. Her cheeks were flushed, whether from his palm or arousal, it was hard to say.

"One thing I'm curious about," Ronan continued as he walked slowly around the naked girl, who had managed to keep her fingers laced behind her head during the exercise. "And that's how comfortable you are with your body. With exposing yourself in ways that might please your Master."

"My body is yours, Sir, to command as you see fit."

Ronan nodded, her words like fingers circling his cock. An idea suddenly leaped into his mind, fueled by the memory of a trainer's critique from Hailey's time at The Compound. It would be most interesting to see how she'd progressed in that regard. Excited, he snapped, "Drop your arms. Go over to the spanking bench. Position yourself on the bench so you are kneeling, ass in the air, forehead down."

He followed her as she moved to the bench, admiring the slight sway of her hips. Her ass was small but nicely rounded, an excellent target for a whip or cane, or his bare hand. She assumed the position on her knees, her forehead pressed against the soft leather. He hadn't given her instruction regarding her hands, and she folded them prettily at the base of her back, wrists crossed, fingers relaxed.

Ronan crouched beside her, awed at the awareness of his extraordinary power over another human being, power she'd willingly given him. He placed his hand on her back, palm flat. Hailey tensed slightly at his touch. He moved his hand slowly up her spine, pressing lightly against the supple muscles with his fingers until he felt her tension ease.

Now for the test.

He removed his hand and scooted around so he was directly behind her. "Reach back and spread your ass cheeks. Lift your ass higher and show me your asshole."

Though he couldn't see her face, she didn't react immediately—cause for punishment, but for now he let it pass as he waited to see what she would do. She let out a breath and slowly moved her hands, finally bringing them to rest on her pretty little bottom.

She reached for her ass cheeks and pulled them apart. Ronan could feel her hesitation as if it were a force field between them, but she did finally do as she was told.

He moved behind her and, licking his finger, touched the little asterisk. "This is an area of sensitivity for you," he remarked. He pushed his finger into the tight opening. "Tell me, Hailey. Do you like anal sex?"

He knew the answer from her slave portfolio, but wanted to hear her say it.

"If it pleases you, Sir. My body is yours."

He pushed the finger in deeper. "I'm not asking about my pleasure or my property. Answer the question as asked. Do you like anal sex?"

She hesitated and then said, haltingly, "Y-yes, Sir. I like the submissive aspect of it."

Ronan cocked an eyebrow and grinned to himself. Good save. She hadn't lied, at least not precisely. He believed her statement, as far as it went. He had asked the wrong question. He clarified. "Do you like the feel of something inside your ass? A cock, say, or a butt plug?"

"No, Sir," she whispered. "Not really."

"Not really?" He moved his finger inside her ass. "What does that mean? Either you do, or you don't."

"I have a hard time relaxing, Sir. I'm not really sure why. But when I tense up, it...it hurts, Sir."

"It hurts?" Ronan chuckled. "But you're a masochist. Pain is a good thing."

"Yes, Sir. Certain types of pain, yes. I just—I don't know. I have a hard time with it. My trainer at The Compound said I have, uh, issues with my asshole, Sir. He said I still required work in that area. I'm—I'm sorry, Sir."

Tenderness suffused him, along with a kind of admiration. Would he ever be able to make himself as vulnerable to another person as this girl so willingly made herself for him? "No need to apologize," he said gently. "I appreciate your honesty, Hailey. Your issue with anal play is something we can work on together, you and I." He withdrew his finger.

"But right now, I have something else in mind. I made a very exciting purchase recently, something I've been looking to acquire for quite some time. You get to be my first subject." He tapped her shoulder, a gesture he was aware was used routinely at The Compound to signal to a slave they should rise from their position.

She lifted herself from the bench and stood beside him. He noted the flush on her cheeks and neck, and knew the exercise had been a difficult one for her. He tucked the knowledge away as he led her to his most recent acquisition, which enjoyed pride of place along the center of one wall.

"Know what that is?"

~*~

"Not exactly, Sir." Hailey stared at the wooden frame with its roller, bars and manacles, relieved the focus had shifted from her asshole. "Some kind of torture device?" she guessed.

"That's right. It's a rack. A medieval torture rack like the kind used in the Inquisition to get poor bastards to confess—well, to confess to anything at all, whether it was true or not." Ronan led her closer, as stories she had read in history texts about heretics put to the rack took on a new and immediate meaning.

"This is a replica, of course, but a very good one. Do you know how it works?"

"No, Sir," Hailey said, both intrigued and frightened by the ominous device.

"The subject's wrists are fastened to this roller, here" — he touched the wooden roller at the top of the rack that spanned the width of the frame, indicating the cuffs secured by chains on either side — "and her ankles are chained like so." He pointed to the cuffs affixed on sidebars at the bottom of the frame.

"During the Inquisition, as the interrogation progressed," Ronan continued, putting his hand on a metal lever attached to one side of the roller, "the torturer would use this handle to gradually increase the tension on the chains. After a certain point, the effect was excruciatingly painful." He turned the handle, and the roller slowly rotated on its axis.

Hailey's mouth was suddenly dry, her heart skittering like a trapped mouse in her chest. At the same time, her cunt was throbbing, her nipples still tingling from Master Ronan's recent touch.

"Being stretched on the rack was bad enough," he went on, a cruel, sensual smile on his handsome face, "but that was just the beginning." They stood side-by-side facing the rack. Ronan put his arm around her shoulders, his hand dropping casually to one breast. His fingers found her nipple, which immediately stiffened in response. Though she'd meant to remain still, she found herself leaning in to his touch. If they'd been lovers, she would have turned to him and pulled his face down to hers for a kiss.

But of course they were not lovers, and she held herself still. She kept her eyes on the rack as Master Ronan continued to weave his dark spell around her. "Once they had the prisoner confined in her chains, her naked body stretched to the breaking point," he murmured, dipping his head so his words tickled her ear, "things would go from bad to worse, the torture only limited by the imaginations of the interrogators. This could include the usual methods of flogging or whipping the bound subject, and if the desired confession still wasn't obtained, might progress to burning the prisoner's flanks with torches, or using pincers made with specially designed grips to tear out finger and toenails."

His arm remained around her shoulders, his fingers still toying with her nipple. "As you might imagine," he murmured, "the prisoner would admit to pretty much anything her tormentors wanted to avoid that kind of pain."

He let her go and turned to face her. "Hey," he chided with a grin, "don't look so terrified. I'm not nearly as sadistic as those misguided fanatics. As we both understand, erotic torture bears little in common with that barbaric treatment. For those of us hardwired like you and me, the pleasure and the erotic pain, the power and the submission, intertwine into something..." He paused, as if searching for the word.

Sublime, Hailey thought, though she didn't volunteer the word since he hadn't given her permission to speak.

"Sublime," he said with a sudden smile, as if somehow she'd managed to send the word directly into his brain. Despite her trepidation about being placed on the rack, Hailey found herself smiling back.

Ronan stepped closer to the rack and turned toward her. His eyes were glittering in a way that at once thrilled and terrified her. "Come here. It's time."

Hailey's breath hiccupped in her throat and she had to make a concerted effort to calm herself. Up until that moment she had instinctively trusted her new Master, but suddenly she felt unsure. They were alone on his property. Yes, others knew she was there, but no one would think to inquire or interfere, not for some time. What if, instead of a dedicated Master seeking a sincere experience with a trained submissive, Ronan Wolfe was actually a madman?

As if called up by her turmoil, George's kind face loomed in her mind. It was clear from the brief interaction she'd witnessed between the two men that they were close friends. George wouldn't be friends with a madman. Would he?

And then she remembered Ronan's kiss, and afterward the way he had looked at her with such naked yearning she'd had to catch her breath, and the fear slipped back into its proper place of erotic anticipation. He was just doing that thing sensual sadists did. She was familiar enough with her trainers' tactics in creating an atmosphere. Ronan was doing the same thing.

And this was what she had wanted, wasn't it? What she had worked so hard at The Compound to achieve. She was no longer playing at BDSM. This wasn't the intense but ultimately staged environment at The Compound. This was the real thing. She had given herself to another person, willingly and without reservation or recourse. The fear of the unknown could be worked through. In fact, it was part of the process, part of finally becoming who and what she was born to be.

Thus newly resolved, she stepped up onto the wooden plank at the base of the rack.

"Lean your back against the frame so you're facing me," Master Ronan instructed. As she obeyed, Hailey wondered if he could hear her heartbeat, which thundered in her ears.

He moved closer. "Spread your legs so your ankles are at the cuffs."

Hailey glanced down and positioned her ankles on either side of the frame, watching as her new Master knelt and wrapped them snugly into place, securing them with Velcro closures.

He rose and stepped back. "Now your wrists."

Hailey lifted her arms and rested her wrists against the open leather cuffs that dangled by chains from the roller on either side. Ronan closed the cuffs around each wrist and then reached for the handle to the left of the roller. He turned it slowly. As it moved, the chains at both sets of cuffs tightened, stretching Hailey's body into a taut X.

At first the feeling was purely sensual — the rush of release and pleasure she always felt when properly bound. Then he turned it once more, and her muscles and tendons strained against the tension. He was watching her carefully. She felt faint, her heart beating wildly. He turned the handle once more, and her shoulder and knee joints popped softly. She yelped without meaning to.

Shit! Was she going to have to use her safeword so soon?

But he had let go of the handle. He moved in front of her and placed his hands over her breasts, cupping them. "Shh," he said soothingly. "Shh, slow down. Breathe. You're okay, Hailey."

As she caught her breath, Hailey realized she was, indeed, okay. True, she was stretched more tautly than she'd ever been, but she was extremely limber due to her yoga training, and her muscles and tendons seemed to be adapting to the tension.

Ronan leaned closer, his lips brushing hers with just the hint of a kiss that nearly had her begging for more. He leaned away, his hands still cupping her breasts. He must have been able to feel the pounding of her heart. "That's as far as I'll go with the roller. I would never harm you."

He moved his hands from her breasts, trailing them down her stomach to her thighs. He cupped her cunt with his right hand and stroked the heat between her spread legs. She was unable to stop the low, feral moan of pure lust his touch wrenched from her lips. His smile as he stared into her eyes was a knowing one, and she felt the heat of a blush flame over her face and neck.

"You're wet, slave Hailey. Did you know that?"

Her face still hot, Hailey nodded and then forced herself to answer. "Yes, Sir."

"Why are you wet, slave?"

Hailey blew out a breath. "Because I'm bound to the rack, Sir. It's that feeling of being held down, the giving over of myself. I'm—I feel helpless, erotically helpless." *And because you're about the sexiest man I've ever been with. No. I can't say that.* "It's hard to explain but—"

He touched her lips with two fingers. "You just did. Perfectly. And I understand. I am the flip side of your coin, Hailey. As you were born to this, so was I. We both get it. I know what you need. Not just what you want. And I plan to give it to you."

He stepped back, and though she couldn't move even a fraction of an inch, Hailey strained in her bonds, her cunt throbbing, her nipples aching with longing for this man she'd only just met.

She could see the outline of his cock, long and hard beneath the white cotton shorts. His legs were strong, his stomach flat, his shoulders and chest smooth and broad. No wonder women swooned over this guy. And yet, while clearly masterful, he didn't come off as an arrogant creep. How in the world had she gotten so lucky?

She watched as he went to the wall that contained the floggers and whips. She hoped he would choose the flogger, her favorite. Her skin began to tingle in anticipation of its sensual, all-encompassing caress. But when he returned, Master Ronan was holding a cane.

He released some kind of lever at the base of the rack and pushed the apparatus, causing the whole thing to tilt back, lifting Hailey from a standing position to a forty-five degree angle above the ground. The disorienting effect of her new position was heightened by the taut stretch of her limbs and her complete inability to move a muscle.

Standing beside her, he ran the edge of the long, thin cane along her stomach and tapped her breasts lightly with the tip. "Do you like the cane, slave Hailey?"

"Yes, Sir." A tremor rippled through her core. *Like* was such an inadequate word to describe how she felt about being caned.

As if reading her mind, Master Ronan supplemented, "You're a masochist, and you have a love-hate relationship with the cane, am I right?"

"Yes, Sir."

"You thrill to its anticipatory swish in the split second before it lands, aching to feel its cleansing, sharp cut. But when it actually hits, the pain is excruciating—you can't take it. And yet you do. And a moment later the pain eases into something deep and powerful, something that grabs hold of you and pulls you into its dark, erotic embrace. And you want another. And another. And another."

"Oooh," Hailey breathed, stunned at the picture his words were creating, amazed he understood so well.

"I know," he whispered, his eyes blazing. "I know." He stepped back and raised his cane arm. "I'm going to cane you now, slave. I'm going to take your measure. You will thank me for each stroke. And if you want more, you will ask me for another. Understood?"

"Yes, Sir."

"Relax your hands."

Hailey realized she had unwittingly clenched her hands into fists. She forced her fingers to uncurl.

"We begin."

The first cut landed across both thighs. No gentle warming of the skin with the light tapping she was used to during caning sessions at The Compound. Just one brutal crack and then the sharp, cutting pain.

"Thank you, Sir!" Hailey cried, remembering his instruction just in time. She was breathing shallowly, and she forced herself to take a deep breath, the air shuddering through her and then easing as she blew it out. Precisely as he'd described, the pain had shifted into a dark, perfect craving, and she begged, "Please, Sir. May I have another?"

"Yes."

The second stroke landed slightly higher than the first, the tip of the cane hitting her hipbone and sending a stinging jolt through her that emerged from her lips as a cry. She felt the sweat breaking out on her forehead and beneath her arms. She swallowed hard and managed, "Thank you, Sir. Please...may I have another?"

"You may."

The third stroke hit the tender flesh of her abdomen and she groaned. "Thank you, Sir. Please, may I have another?"

She expected the next cut to land on her breasts, but instead the stroke seared across her left thigh. A rapid second stroke landed on the right. "Oh god," she breathed. *I can't do it. But I have to. I can't let him down. I want it. But I hate it. I want to be let off this thing. I want to suck his cock. I'm thirsty.*

"Focus," Master Ronan warned.

Focus. The word cut through the jumble of her unruly thoughts.

She was supposed to do something. Say something. Her skin was on fire, her joints and muscles aching, her heart pounding, her cunt throbbing, her senses whirling.

Focus!

Finally she remembered, and belatedly cried, "Thank you, Sir!" She swallowed and twisted to look at her tormentor. He was watching her intently, the cane poised in his hand. Waiting.

She knew what he wanted. Did she want it?

She did.

"Please, Sir. May I have another?"

"With pleasure."

This time he struck the underside of her left breast, the blow gentler than the others had been, but it still hurt like hell against the tender skin. She hissed her pain, then managed her thanks. As much as it hurt, her right breast was aching for the symmetry of a like cut, and she asked for it. "Please, Sir. May I have another?"

He obliged, searing her second breast with the cracking cut of the cane. A trickle of sweat rolled down her back. The welts she couldn't see but certainly could feel undulated over her skin like fiery snakes. At the same time, her cunt ached and she silently begged her new Master to climb on top of her and fill her with his hard, perfect cock.

"Slave. You are forgetting yourself."

His words startled her and for one terrified second she was afraid she'd accidentally uttered her wanton thoughts aloud. Then she realized what she'd forgotten and hastily said, "Thank you, Sir."

"And?"

Did she want another?

Yes.

She asked.

This time the cane hit the upper side of one breast, and then the other in rapid succession. "Fuck," Hailey whispered, and then blushed, the word not usually part of her active vocabulary. In a louder voice, she cried, "Thank you, Sir," and before giving herself a chance to think about it, added, "May I have another?"

The stroke to her nipple made her see stars, and she heard herself scream. She knew if she had been standing, she would have fallen to the ground at that moment, her hands clutching her throbbing nipple. It was too much. Too much.

But all she could do was open and close her hands as she struggled to maintain what was left of her decorum. "Thank you, Sir," she finally managed to croak.

She knew he was waiting.

I'm going to take your measure.

This was a test—her first test. She would not fail. "Please, Sir," she said, the sound of her words faint in her own ears. "May I have another?"

"Yes."

The second nipple exploded in a ripple of radiating pain and a sob burst from Hailey's mouth. She pressed her lips together and blinked back tears.

"Thank you, Sir," she whispered.

Her eyes were closed, but they flew open when she felt his mouth close lightly over her nipple, his tongue licking away the pain. He lifted his head and lowered it again on her second nipple, again kissing away the worst of the pain.

"You please me, slave girl," he murmured. He stepped back and to the side of the rack. She heard a clicking sound she recognized as the lever release. He pushed against the rack until it was parallel to the ground so she faced the ceiling, which was comprised of rough, bare wooden beams.

Master Ronan ran his fingers lightly over the welts he had left on her body. His hand trailed down between her legs, his fingers once again finding her spread cunt and slipping inside. "You're soaking wet," he announced, and Hailey closed her eyes, embarrassed her lust was so obvious, even though she recalled his mandate that she always be wet and ready for him.

Now the question was, would he do anything about it?

He answered the unspoken question with a circle of his fingers up and over her clit, which throbbed and twitched to his touch. He moved his fingers teasingly over her sex until she started to tremble. Oh god, was he going to let her come? He pressed his palm against her clit as his fingers explored the tight heat inside her. She began to pant. As he moved his hand against her, he leaned over to kiss and suckle her breasts.

She felt the delicious, buttery sensation of a climax sliding over her. What was the protocol? He hadn't said...oh god, it was so good. So fucking good. Oh...ohhh...

"Please, Sir," she finally managed to gasp. "May I come?"

The hand fell away. The lips were withdrawn.

Hailey opened her eyes in dismay and bit her lip to keep from swearing again in her frustration. She forced herself to look at her new Master. He was smiling, a cruel glint in his eyes. "Have you earned it, slave Hailey?"

She hated that question. She never knew how to answer it.

He must have taken her hesitation as a no, because he shook his head and said, "No, I agree. You haven't yet earned the right to an orgasm. We'll need to work on your focus." He smiled again and shrugged. "But that's okay. I don't expect perfection. After all, it's only your first day."

He pushed the rack slowly downward until she was again standing upright. Crouching in front of her, he released her ankles from the cuffs. Suddenly exhausted, she sagged in her restraints. He put one arm supportively around her waist as he undid first one wrist cuff and then the other. She fell against him and he took her into his arms. If she pretended to be a little weaker than she actually was, it was only so he would continue to hold her.

He lifted her from the platform and set her on her feet. His arm still around her, he walked her to the tiny bedroom. He left her standing a moment as he pushed the coil of chain out of the way. He guided her down to the bed. It was surprisingly comfortable, the sheets fresh and cool.

He knelt beside her and examined her wrists and ankles, apparently satisfied there was no lasting damage from the restraints. He ran his finger lightly over the welts on her breasts, stomach and thighs. His touch reignited the sexual fire still burning inside her, but he was all business, his expression one of caretaker, not lover.

"Those aren't too severe," he informed her, his tone clinical. "We didn't break the skin. But just to be safe, I'll put a little salve on them."

He rose and went into the bathroom, returning a moment later carrying a cup of water and a tube of salve, the same kind they used at The Compound. Hailey lifted her head and Master Ronan tilted the cup to her lips, letting her drink her fill. "Thank you, Sir," she murmured, her head falling heavily back to the pillow.

She closed her eyes and let out a contented sigh as he gently rubbed the soothing cream into her tender, abraded skin. She hadn't realized until that moment just how wiped out she was. The fatigue of the last day of travel and the whirlwind of her first few hours in Master Ronan's charge had left her bone weary. Master Ronan was saying something about food and rest, but she couldn't focus on his words. She didn't have the strength left to lift a finger, much less keep her eyes open.

She heard the clank of the chain, and was dimly aware of something being attached to her collar, but was too exhausted to investigate. Despite the lingering ache in her unrequited cunt, she felt herself sinking into a dark, warm pool of slumber. She opened her mouth, intending to thank Master Ronan for the session, but before the words were out, she was gone.

Chapter 4

A small pinging sound indicated movement and Ronan's gaze shifted from the ocean to the iPad he'd set on the patio table. Hailey was stirring at last. She hadn't moved for the past hour, and he had been considering waking her soon, though clearly she needed the rest. He was glad she was waking of her own accord. She must be hungry. He would pull out one of the many dishes his cook had prepared before he'd sent her on a week's paid vacation. His slave girl needed her strength, after all.

His slave girl!

Was this really happening?

The timing was perfect. His schedule was clear for the foreseeable future. There were no looming interviews, no scripts to read, no shoots to retake. His latest movie was in post-production, and he was in no hurry to move on to the next project, despite his agent's constant pressure to seize the moment while he was still "hot".

Hailey rolled from her side to her back. As she looked around the small space, he waited to see if she'd spy the unobtrusive home security camera he'd placed in a high corner, angled to take in the entire room. She didn't seem to notice it, her eyes focusing instead on the skylight overhead.

Ronan had spent a night in the small bedroom in anticipation of her arrival to make sure the accommodations were suitable. He'd even placed a collar around his neck and slept in the chain. Its clanking had awakened him a few times as he turned over in his sleep, but otherwise the night had passed peacefully enough. He'd had to pee sometime before dawn, but had forced himself to hold it, reminding himself his slave girl would be expected to do the same.

She spied the bottle of water he'd placed beside the mattress. Lifting herself on one elbow, she reached for it and twisted off the cap. She drank deeply, replaced the cap and set it again beside the bed. She looked toward the door and called softly, "Master Ronan?"

He would go to her soon, but for the moment he enjoyed just watching her. With a small sigh, she lay back down. She touched her collar and then picked up the chain, letting the links slide through her fingers. She glanced again toward the open door.

Ronan started to rise, eager to see her in the flesh, but her movement on the screen caught his attention once more, and he sat slowly down again.

Her hands were moving over her body, stroking her breasts, tracing the welts still visible from the caning. She brought her knees up so her feet were flat on the mattress and let her legs fall open. He had a perfect view of her smooth, bare cunt, the delicate labia flowering at her center. His cock stiffened in appreciation. He definitely had to fuck her soon.

Her right hand moved down between her legs. She moaned, the sound low and sexy. Ronan was riveted to the screen. He couldn't possibly be witnessing what he seemed to be, and yet the camera didn't lie.

She lifted her head and looked toward the open door, as if listening. After a moment she let her head fall again to the pillow. Her hand still covered her sex. She closed her eyes and bit her lip. Her hand began moving at her cunt, slowly at first, and then with more urgency.

"What the fuck?" Ronan whispered, both stunned and intrigued. Where was the extraordinarily trained slave girl he'd left chained in her dungeon bed? Surely she hadn't forgotten his direct admonition not to touch herself without his express direction and permission.

"Why, that little slut," he murmured, at once amused and angry. His cock had hardened to full erection at the sight of the masturbating beauty, but that didn't excuse the wanton behavior, nor the flagrant disregard of a direct command.

He waited, his eyes glued to the screen. She began to pant, her breath interspersed with small mewling sounds. She stiffened suddenly and sighed a long, "ooooooh," before going limp.

While aroused by what he'd witnessed, at the same time a small, bright ball of anger burned in Ronan's chest. He felt tricked. Duped. Betrayed the moment his back was turned. The anger mingled with a sudden sadness. Maybe there was no such thing as a true submissive.

Hailey opened her eyes and lifted herself again on an elbow, turning to face the doorway. "Shit," she whispered, her face crumpling in anguish. "Oh, shit, shit, shit." She fell heavily back to the mattress and pushed her tousled hair back from her face. Clearly, she knew what she'd just done was wrong—in direct opposition to her Master's dictates.

Closing the iPad cover, Ronan jumped to his feet and strode into the house. He bounded up both flights of stairs and walked rapidly through the dungeon to the girl's room.

"Oh!" she said softly as he entered the small room. "Sir." She swallowed hard and blew out a breath. Her cheeks and chest were still flushed with post-orgasmic color, the guilt writ large on her face.

"You're awake, I see," Ronan said, his voice coming out harder than he'd intended.

"Yes, Sir."

He forced a smile. "Did you rest comfortably?"

"Yes, Sir. I...um..." She bit her lip, her eyes filling with tears.

Ronan moved to her. Crouching beside her, he unclasped the chain from her collar. "Yes? What is it, Hailey? Do you have something to tell me?"

She swallowed hard and blinked back the tears. He could see the struggle in her face but he made no move to intervene. He waited.

"I-I need to use the bathroom, please, Sir."

Ronan frowned, but swallowed his disappointment. "Of course." He gestured toward the bathroom. He rose to his feet as Hailey rolled from the mattress and stood. She walked a little unsteadily toward the bathroom. He didn't follow.

He waited as he heard her use the toilet and then run the water in the sink. She came out a moment later. "Feeling better?" he asked, still deciding how to play this.

She smiled, but after a moment the smile slid away from her face and tears again filled her eyes. She sank to her knees and lowered herself until her head was touching the floor at his feet. "I'm sorry, Sir. I'm so sorry," she said, her words muffled by her position.

The tight ball of anger melted away. He was nearly certain she remained unaware she'd been watched, and yet she was going to confess! He instantly forgave her, though he wasn't going to let her off the hook.

"What for, Hailey? Why are you sorry?"

She mumbled something into the floor. Ronan crouched in front of her and tapped her shoulder. "Talk to me. Tell me what's going on."

Hailey leaned back on her haunches and wrapped her arms protectively around her torso. A single tear rolled down her cheek. "I disobeyed you, Sir. I didn't mean to. Well, I mean, I didn't quite realize what was happening until it was too late." She pressed her lips together and shook her head, a resolute look coming over her face.

"Okay, no. No, that's not true. I could have stopped. I knew what I was doing. I was just so—" Again she stopped herself. "No. No excuse, Sir. I disobeyed you. I'm so very sorry."

Another tear coursed down her face. Ronan wiped it away with his thumb. "Tell me," he said gently. "Tell me what happened."

She looked down. "I touched myself, Sir. I...I made myself come, Sir."

"I see."

She looked up. "I'm so embarrassed, Sir. I wasn't thinking clearly. I was just so—I mean, you're so, um, I mean, it's been so long and...god, there is no excuse. I disobeyed you. I knew what I was doing."

"And...?"

"And I need to be punished, Sir." Her voice trembled slightly and she looked down at the floor.

"Yes. I agree." Ronan stood, relief, excitement and trepidation moving through him in equal measure.

Though he'd witnessed it several times during his training, he'd never actually punished someone himself for a specific transgression.

"Remind me," he said, looking down at her blond head, "what the punishment is for touching yourself and orgasming without permission."

"I'm to be whipped until you..." she faltered and then continued, "until you draw blood, Sir." Her voice cracked as she said the word *blood*.

"That's correct." He let the statement hang in the air for a while. She was trembling, clearly terrified of what awaited her. She could have kept quiet. He was nearly certain she was unaware of the security camera. Her conscience had driven her to do the right thing, not fear of being called out. She had transgressed, but then she'd faced up to what she'd done, despite the fact that blood seemed to be a negative trigger for her.

For a moment Ronan wavered. It was her first day, after all. She'd been through a lot. Perhaps he should let it go and move on. The words of Henry Schaffer, his primary trainer at The Exchange Club, came into his mind, and he knew that would be the wrong decision. Henry had taught him the importance of never making a promise to a sub on which you weren't fully prepared to follow through. A Master must stand by his word. He owed it not only to himself, but to his submissive.

By the same token, he needed to take proper care of his slave girl. He tapped her shoulder. As she rose to her feet, he said, "You will be punished. But first, you need to eat something. Let's go down and have some dinner."

"Yes, Sir. Thank you, Sir." She offered a tremulous smile.

He couldn't help it. He took her into his arms and kissed her.

~*~

The food was delicious—several fine cheeses and cold meats, and some kind of flaky puff pastry filled with mushrooms, plus little fruit tarts with custard for dessert—but Hailey had a hard time getting much down, anxiety over the upcoming punishment looming large in her mind.

She still couldn't quite believe she'd done what she'd done. Even as she rubbed herself to rapid orgasm, she had known she was breaking the rules, and that she would have to confess.

The real question was why had she done it?

She knew the answer, of course. It was Ronan's fault. Well, not his fault precisely, but she'd been so deeply aroused not only by his physical beauty, but by his intensely masterful domination in their first hours together, coupled with the passion of that one perfect kiss, that she'd been on fire with lust.

She'd let her body's needs override her sense of duty as Master Ronan's submissive. She'd lost her way long enough to steal her own pleasure, in flagrant disregard to her Master's express wishes. It had been a relief to confess, but now she had to face the consequences.

It was odd, too—she'd sensed Master Ronan wavering as he decided how to handle her confession, and in that split second before he announced his decision, she realized she didn't want him to let her off the hook. She understood in that moment she needed a Master who stood by his word, no matter how harsh the decree might be.

Master Ronan pushed back from the table. "You ready, slave girl? It's time."

Hailey set down her fork, her heart doing a loop-de-loop in her chest. "Yes, Sir."

She followed silently behind her Master as he moved through the house and up both sets of stairs. By the time they reached the dungeon, the small amount of food she'd managed to ingest sat like a ball of lead in her belly, and a combination of fear and anticipation rose like a lump in her throat, making it hard to swallow.

Master Ronan led her to the center of the room. He faced her, his hands on his hips. He still wore the white shorts he'd had on earlier, and had put a faded red T-shirt on over them. His feet were still bare. "You will stand for your punishment. I'm not going to restrain you in any way. You will raise your hands over your head and cross your wrists. You will not move until I give you permission to do so. I'm going to whip you until you bleed. Do you agree willingly to this punishment, slave Hailey?"

"Yes, Sir. Thank you, Sir," she managed, fairly certain her voice hadn't trembled. She lifted her arms and crossed her wrists as directed, willing her heartbeat and her breathing to slow.

Serenity. Peace. Submission. Grace.

He left her and went to the whip wall. He returned a moment later with a long signal whip, the leather thong coiled in one hand. He let it unfurl. It was easily three feet long, the last several inches studded with knots.

Hailey drew in a deep, cleansing breath. She could do this. She deserved it. She needed it.

Master Ronan cracked the whip in the air and Hailey jumped.

"I said you are not to move," he snapped.

Hailey was embarrassed at her lack of control. She knew better. "Yes, Sir. Excuse me, Sir. I will do better."

"Prepare yourself. Twenty strokes. I will keep silent count for you."

The first one licked across her left ass cheek, leaving a line of fire in its wake. Hailey pressed her lips together to keep from crying out. She was determined to take her punishment like a woman.

The second one hit her right cheek in the same spot. It was clear he was a master with the signal whip. Despite the pain, she took comfort from this.

The third stroke caught both cheeks at once, the leather cutting like a knife. In spite of her promise to herself, Hailey yelped with pain.

Several more strokes landed on her ass. Through it all, Hailey managed to hold herself in position, though she couldn't quite stifle the little cries each cut of the knotted whip yanked from her lips. Still, she was proud of how she was enduring, and as long as she didn't focus on the thought of her own blood, she could get through this.

Then he struck her back, and all promises of stoic obedience flew out the window. The pain was excruciating—nothing erotic about it. She screamed and stumbled forward.

"Back in position," Master Ronan barked.

Hailey hurried to obey, pushing down the tide of panic threatening to break over her.

Serenity. Peace. Submission. Grace.

She straightened her spine and lifted her chin. She was strong. She was brave. She could do this.

The whip snaked between her shoulder blades and crisscrossed its way down her back. Several times she nearly begged him to stop. Her safeword rose like a prayer to her lips, but she pressed them together to keep it from escaping.

She would not give in. Master Ronan had promised her he would never harm her, and she believed him.

As the knotted leather continued its cruel journey over her skin, somehow she managed to stand tall and still, save for the uncontrollable trembling that had taken over her body. The whip returned to her ass, each stinging stroke like the cut of a knife. Hailey continued to recite her four-word mantra in her head, determined to make it through the ordeal. It had to be nearly over.

When it finally stopped, the pain continued to throb through tortured nerve endings. Sweat stung the skin on her back, ass and thighs. She wanted to sink to the ground and curl into a ball, but she held her position, arms over her head, wrists crossed, feet planted firmly on the ground.

Ronan appeared in front of her. He set the whip on the ground. "You may lower your arms. Stand at ease. The punishment is over. You did well. We move forward now—a clean slate."

Hailey longed to wash herself clean in a cool shower. *Soon,* she told herself. *Soon he will let me. I did well. The slate is clean.*

She watched as Ronan moved to one wall of the dungeon and returned carrying a full-length mirror on its own stand. He set it down behind her.

"Look," he commanded. "See the results of your punishment."

Hailey felt a trickle of something warm and wet roll down her back. The air shimmered suddenly in front of her eyes and the room seemed to tip. She swallowed hard, willing away the rising nausea in her gut at the thought of seeing her own blood. She wanted to refuse, but it hadn't been a question, and she hadn't been offered a choice.

Steeling herself, she twisted back to see the damage. Her back and ass were striped with welts, but, though she'd been convinced he'd cut the skin a dozen times, in fact there were only two small trickles of blood, one just below her left shoulder blade, the other on her right thigh.

Still, those small, seeping red droplets were enough to tip the room again, and make the air swim unsteadily before her eyes. A strange whooshing sound rose in her ears. Ronan's mouth was moving but she couldn't make out the words. She felt herself tumbling forward and then his arms were around her. She closed her eyes and let the world slip away.

When she opened them again, she was lying on her stomach with absolutely no idea where she was or how she got there. She lay there utterly confused for several long seconds, until a deep, masculine voice jerked her back to the present.

"There you are. I was starting to get worried, Hailey."

Hailey turned her head to focus on the man speaking. At the sight of Master Ronan the events of the last hour poured back into her brain like water spilling into a basin. "What happened?" she asked stupidly, her last memory that of twisting back to see herself in the mirror.

"What happened is you passed out cold. No warning. One second you were standing there, the next you were pitching forward, face-first. It was sheer luck I was able to catch you before you hit the ground."

"Wow. Really? How long was I out for?"

"Just a couple of minutes. Are you feeling okay?"

The skin on her back and ass was coming back alive with a stinging vengeance. Other than that, she felt fine. "I'm okay, Sir. I'm sorry I did that. I've always been a little, uh, squeamish at the sight of my own blood."

Ronan lifted a washcloth from a bowl of sudsy water and squeezed out the excess. He touched it lightly to her back and Hailey struggled not to wince. He moved it gently and carefully over her skin. "You should have warned me, Hailey. Blood wasn't listed in your hard limits."

"No, Sir. I'm sorry. I thought I was doing better with that, Sir. I had some training at The Compound. I don't know what happened. It just—I'm sorry."

He dipped the washcloth, wrung it out and again began to gently clean her skin. It felt good and she closed her eyes. "Okay," he said. "But you need to talk to me, okay? One of the keys of any relationship, D/s or otherwise, is communication. I realize some of this is my fault. By telling you only to speak when spoken to, I limited your ability to communicate. I want to change that rule a little right now."

Hailey opened her eyes as she waited for him to continue. Ronan dropped the washcloth in the water. Using a hand towel, he carefully blotted her skin. Next he smoothed the healing salve over the welts. His touch and his aftercare felt good.

"I want you to feel freer to speak," he said, "especially if you're afraid of something, or uncertain. You should know that I plan to take you further and deeper than your training at The Compound. I've been training too, you see. For over a year, I've been working with Master Dominants at a highly specialized BDSM training facility."

Hailey opened her eyes in surprise. Though she knew the trainers at The Compound received some kind of formal BDSM education, it honestly hadn't occurred to her that her new Master would have done the same. She realized she'd just assumed he'd bought her contract because he could.

Seeing the evident surprise on her face, Ronan smiled. "I take my position as your Master every bit as seriously as you take yours as my slave. I've had a lifelong fascination with the scene, and before I got too famous to go out in public without being assaulted, I used to go to clubs, but it has only been in the past few years that my interest has became more serious."

He finished applying the salve, and Hailey felt the loss of his touch, though of course she kept this to herself. "Thank god for George," Ronan continued. "He's the one who told me about The Exchange. That's the club where I received my training."

Hailey nodded to show she was listening. "So, yeah," Ronan continued, "back to what I was saying before — I want you to feel free to communicate when you've got issues, because I plan to — what did your contract say?" He looked up at the ceiling, as if reading some words he'd written there earlier. "Oh yeah — press the envelope of your submission as far as I deem appropriate." He paused and then added, "And that's pretty far, so consider yourself warned." He laughed, the sound at once sensual and cruel, and a shiver of raw desire hurtled through Hailey's loins.

He tapped her shoulder. "You okay to sit up? I thought we could go out and sit by the ocean for a while. The sun's setting about now. This is my favorite time of the evening."

He helped her to a sitting position and then stood, extending a hand. She took it, allowing him to pull her to her feet. "You good?" he inquired.

"Yes, thank you, Sir. I'm fine now."

He nodded. "Good. So here's the new rule. You may speak at any time you feel frightened or threatened in any way by what I'm asking you to do.

In fact, I want you to, especially during this first month as we get to know each other. I will listen to your concerns." He grinned, flashing his white movie-star smile. "Not that it means I'll necessarily stop what I'm doing." The smile fell away, though his mesmerizing green eyes continued to dance.

"In all seriousness, this exploration between us will be a two-way street. I do plan to push that envelope of yours further than you might think you can go, but I've already got a sense of your courage and your determination, and I like what I see."

"Thank you, Sir," Hailey said, the warmth of his praise moving through her like sunlight.

"That said"—he grinned again as he led her through the dungeon—"no more touching my property without permission." He playfully swatted her mons, and her clit leaped to instant attention. "Got it?"

"Got it, Sir," she replied, looking away so he wouldn't see her blush.

Chapter 5

The sky was pink and white, the edges glimmering with molten gold. The water was silver and through his open windows Ronan could hear the waves gently lapping at the sand on his private beach. He loved this time of morning, before the hustle of the world, with its steady stream of texting, phone calls, appointments and obligations smashed through the peace like an iron fist through glass.

He touched the sleeping iPad beside him and the image of his slave girl lying naked and in chains appeared on the screen. Her room was bathed in the lemony half-light of dawn pouring through her skylight. As if feeling his eyes on her, she rolled from her side to her back, her eyes opening. Her hands moved to the collar around her neck, and then her fingers slid down the length of the chain one link at a time, as if it were a rosary. Her lips moved and he strained to catch the sound, but heard only the faint clink of the chain.

He glanced at the clock. It was only five thirty. He had planned to let her sleep as late as she liked this morning, since she'd had a long and exhausting first day. His cock hardened as he thought about what lay in store today. Now wide awake, he swung his legs over the side of the bed and stood. He picked up the iPad and carried it with him to the bathroom. After peeing and washing up, he glanced again at the iPad screen. She was still awake, eyes focused on the skylight. Her hands were under her head, elbows jutting out on either side. What was she thinking?

Ronan toweled himself dry and padded into the bedroom. Grabbing his shorts, he slid them on and headed out of the room, eager to greet his slave. She must have heard him coming, because when he entered the room, she was on her knees on the mattress, palms resting upward on her spread thighs, back straights, eyes down, the chain falling in a line between her breasts, the very picture of submissive repose.

"Good morning, slave Hailey," Ronan said. "Did you sleep well?"

"Yes, Sir. Thank you, Sir."

"I saw you were already awake, so I figured we'd go ahead and get the day started."

Her eyes flew up to meet his. "You saw? I'm sorry, what?"

He grinned. So she still didn't know. He pointed to the small, round camera nestled in shadow in the corner and watched the dawning realization on her face. "Did you think I'd leave you shackled and alone without making sure you were safe? I can see and hear you from wherever I am with that security camera. Audio and video, as sensitive as a baby monitor, but less obvious."

Her mouth had fallen open, and a red flush moved over her cheeks like a wash of paint. Her hand flew to her mouth to cover a small, "Oh!" Recalling herself, she quickly lowered her hand back to her thigh and dropped her eyes.

"That's right," Ronan said, unable to hide his smile. "I knew what you'd done yesterday before you admitted it. It took real strength of character for you to confess without knowing I had seen your hand buried in that hot little cunt of yours."

"Oh, Sir," she murmured, the words ripe with contrition. "I'm so sorry —"

He moved closer and put his hand on the top of her head. "Stop. You transgressed. You confessed. You were punished, and it's over. I told you that. We move forward. I need for you to let go of that, okay? Can you do that for me, Hailey?"

She looked up at him with grateful eyes. "Yes, Sir. Thank you, Sir."

He squatted beside her and undid the clip that attached the chain to her collar. He had considered the idea of padlocking her at night, but in the event of a possible emergency where he couldn't get to her in time, had decided against it. The collar and chain were symbols of her servitude, nothing more.

"You may use the bathroom and freshen up. You'll find razors and baby oil and whatever else you need in the drawers under the sink. I expect you to groom daily, though I imagine with your level of training, that goes without saying." He rose again to his feet. "Meet me down in the kitchen. We'll go over duties and expectations, and then get the day started."

"Yes, Sir," she replied.

Down in the kitchen, Ronan put on the coffee and pulled out some frozen sweet rolls already on an oven-ready tray. The kitchen had French doors that opened onto a patio overlooking the beach. Coffee mug in hand, he stepped outside to enjoy the air and the view while he waited for his slave to appear.

He was lost in a daydream, lulled by the movement of the ocean, when he heard, "Good morning, Sir." He looked back to see Hailey, naked save for the slave collar around her neck. Her hair was wet, her face free of makeup. There were still faint welts visible on her breasts and thighs.

"Come out here and let me look at you," Ronan said. She stepped out with a glance toward the beach. Though she was too well trained to voice any concern, Ronan offered, "Don't worry, there's nobody out there. This beach is private. It's just us, the dolphins and the gulls." As if to emphasize the point, a white gull wheeled nearby, its beak looking as if it had been dipped in black paint. Ronan waved his hand in its direction. "Get out of here," he called with a laugh. "Nothing to eat, you old scavenger."

The bird flew away with a caw of disappointment. Ronan turned back to his girl. She was already standing at attention, hands behind her head. Excellent. "Turn around so I can see your back and ass," he directed. Hailey pirouetted slowly. There were more welts, thinner but darker than the ones on her front. The two cuts to the skin had scabbed a little, but weren't deep. There was some bruising on her ass.

The awareness that he had done that to her made his cock hard. The knowledge he could do whatever he wanted to her, and she would not only submit, but craved what he could give her, made him harder still. Images of Hailey, naked and bound on the sand, floated into his mind's eye. He would add to those welts and bruises until she begged for mercy. There was no one and nothing to stop him.

The ding of the oven timer brought him back to reality. He pushed back from the table and rose to his feet. Grabbing his mug, he said, "Let's get some breakfast and discuss logistics."

Hailey followed him inside. He turned off the timer and pulled open the oven door. He took out the rolls, inhaling the warm, yeasty scent of Bella's homemade peach sweet rolls. Placing the cookie sheet on the stove, he reached for a second mug and turned to Hailey. "Coffee?"

"Yes, please, Sir."

He poured her a cup and handed it to her. "Have a seat," he said, gesturing toward a barstool. "Cream and sugar are right there." She took her cup and settled herself gingerly on the edge of the leather stool. Ronan transferred the sweet rolls to a plate, refreshed his coffee, and moved with the plate and mug around the counter to sit beside Hailey.

"After this morning," he said, sliding a roll onto a smaller plate and placing it in front of Hailey, "I will expect you to be downstairs before me. You will wake with the sun, as you did today, and you will shower, groom yourself and come directly to the kitchen to make coffee. You are free to enjoy a cup inside or outside until I come down. I'm usually up a little later than this, but not much."

He took a bite of the roll, washed it down with a sip of coffee, and continued, "I gave my chef and cleaning staff the week off to give us time to get acquainted without distraction." He smiled. "During this week, I will expect you to take over basic cleaning and food prep duties. I'll show you where everything is after breakfast, and what I require." He couldn't hide the smile of anticipation as he said this. He really didn't give a damn if the sheets were fresh or the floor swept, but he'd always enjoyed the fantasy of a sexy maid dressed only in high heels and a little frilly skirt, ankles hobbled with a slave chain, on her knees scrubbing the floor with a toothbrush.

"I will inspect your work, and of course you will be punished if things aren't to my liking. Before we get started, I'll show you your uniform." He grinned with anticipation.

He took another sip of coffee. Hailey hadn't touched the roll on her plate. "Aren't you hungry?"

"I am, Sir. Thank you." She picked up the roll and took a bite. "It's delicious, Sir."

"Bella's a fabulous cook. Do you cook?"

"Yes, Sir."

"Good." He nodded and patted his stomach with a grin. "I like to eat."

She smiled. "Permission to speak, Sir?"

"Of course."

"I practice yoga. I find it very relaxing and helpful to do my exercises early in the morning, Sir, usually before I do anything else. Would that be a problem, Sir? I brought my yoga mat and I could do it in my room, or — "

"Oh, shit!" Ronan interrupted, slapping his forehead. "I knew that! I read it in your portfolio." He jumped up from his stool. "I have a surprise for you. Come outside. I'll show you."

He walked quickly through the house to the back veranda and pulled open the doors. Hailey followed him outside and he pointed to the structure he'd made just for her.

"Oh," Hailey breathed, hers eyes shining. "That's perfect."

Ronan beamed with pride. "I was a carpenter before I got into acting," he said. "I still love to work with my hands. This was George's idea, actually. Back when we were first looking at your portfolio and we saw you were heavily into yoga, he thought it might be a nice idea if you had your own dedicated space."

Hailey walked to the simple cabana-like structure Ronan had fashioned, using bamboo for the frame. It was facing the water, the roof and three walls made from white canvas that blocked the sun but still let in the light. A thick yoga mat was set on the ground inside the structure. As an afterthought, Ronan had hung a crystal prism from the ceiling that cast rainbow patterns over the canvas walls.

Ronan moved to stand beside her. "You can do your yoga in the mornings before I come down. And during your free time."

"Thank you, Master Ronan." Hailey dropped to her knees and kissed the tops of Ronan's feet with soft lips.

He clenched his hands into fists as he forced himself to resist the impulse to pull her into his arms and then lower her to the ground. His cock perked, a drop of pre-come wetting his shorts as his imagination had him already on top of her, his shaft buried to the hilt inside her, her arms pinned over her head, his mouth covering hers.

When he'd been studying her portfolio and those of the other potential slave girls George had provided for him, he'd promised himself he wouldn't succumb to the feminine charms of a girl who, once the six month contract was up, would be gone. He needed to be careful going forward. He didn't want to give slave Hailey the wrong impression.

~*~

The yoga meditation left Hailey peaceful and ready to face whatever challenges the day held. Or so she thought until Master Ronan held up the anal plug.

"We're going to work on your ass issues," he announced as she knelt before him in the dungeon. "As one of the steps in working toward desensitization, you'll be wearing a butt plug every day during your chores. We'll start with this relatively small one, and work our way up."

Hailey had been required to wear an anal plug for an entire week at The Compound, removed only for her to use the bathroom. She had learned to accommodate the full feeling, but was still shy about undue attention paid to her bottom. She submitted to inspection and scrutiny, of course, but still remained profoundly uncomfortable with the whole thing. She wished Master Ronan hadn't chosen this particular issue to work on, but then, it wasn't up to her.

He approached her, a tube of lubricant and the plug in hand. "Head down, ass up," he ordered. "Maintain your position while I insert it."

Hailey lowered her head until her forehead rested on the carpet. She closed her eyes, mustering what remained of the lingering yoga peace. She flinched slightly when she felt the cold, gooey blob of lubricant squirted between her cheeks. A moment later she felt his finger rim the hole and then gently press its way inside.

In spite of her trepidation, she had to admit his finger felt good, and her clit perked up, eager for the same attention. But of course, Master Ronan had other plans. His finger was removed, and she felt the hard press of rubber against her sphincter. The plug slid in fairly easily, widening the opening as it moved deeper.

"Stay relaxed," he said from behind her. "This is the last bit." Then came the sudden, sharp pain as the flared end of the plug slipped inside her. It subsided quickly as her anal muscles adjusted to the invading girth.

He tapped her shoulder and she rose back onto her haunches. "Stand up," he commanded. He brought the full-length mirror closer and instructed her to look back at herself. She did, squinting a little with dismay at the sight of the black circle of rubber protruding between her ass cheeks. Then she noticed the bruises and lingering welts, and she drew in her breath.

Badges of courage, one of her trainers had called the marks, and she had to agree. She reached back and touched the cut just below her ass, recalling the wicked stroke of Master Ronan's signal whip. To think, he'd known all along she'd masturbated without permission. How much worse the punishment might have been if she hadn't confessed of her own accord!

"Let's go down now to the cleaning closet." Master Ronan's words snapped her back to the moment. She followed him out of the dungeon and down to the first floor. He pulled open a door next to the powder room, revealing shelves filled with cleaning supplies, brooms and mops neatly lining one wall. A top-of-the-line vacuum stood next to them.

Master Ronan took a shoebox from the bottom shelf and opened it. He removed a pair of shiny red high heels and a short chain with leather cuffs attached on either side. "You will wear these shoes and ankle cuffs while working. They, along with the plug, will remind you of your status as my personal slave. It pleases me to see you suffer. You do understand that, don't you, slave Hailey?"

His cock had hardened visibly beneath his shorts, and his sea glass green eyes glittered with lust. Hailey's nipples leaped to answering attention and she could barely catch her breath enough to reply, "It pleases me to suffer for you, Sir."

"Good. I would expect no less." He set the shoes on the floor and pointed to them. Hailey slipped one foot and then the other into the heels. Until she'd gone to The Compound, Hailey had never worn anything higher a half-inch heel, but the grace and decorum work she'd received during her training served her well now, and she stood tall without a wobble.

Ronan crouched in front of her and secured the cuffs around each ankle. There was give enough for her to walk, but just barely. Cleaning was going to be awkward, but she supposed that was the point. A slave learned to be graceful no matter the challenge placed before her.

Ronan took a small black apron trimmed with white lace from a hook on the inside of the door and told her to put it on, which Hailey did. He went over the duties of scrubbing the bathrooms, making his bed, vacuuming and sweeping, and cleaning the kitchen. "Some days I might give you a special task, but for today just focus on the basics. I may come in and distract you from time to time. You are to ignore me as best you can. That is, don't let it interfere with your work. No matter what I do to you, you remain focused on your task. Are we quite clear on this, slave Hailey?"

"Yes, Sir."

"Good. I leave you to it, then. I have a few things to attend to in my study. I'll come find you when I'm ready."

He strode away. Hailey stood uncertainly for a moment, and then faced the closet. She would do the master bathroom first, and work from upstairs to down. She grabbed a pail, some cleaning supplies, a pair of rubber gloves, a mop and a broom. It was slow going up the stairs in those heels with all her gear in tow and her feet hobbled by the chain. Her cunt throbbed gently and she enjoyed a brief fantasy of rubbing herself to another orgasm once she got upstairs, just to take the edge off, but she knew she would not. One stolen orgasm had been enough. Master Ronan would reward her when he was ready — when she had earned it.

She had finished the master bathroom and was in the process of making Ronan's bed when she heard him coming up the stairs. Recalling his instruction, she didn't stop her work or turn around when she heard him enter the room.

She jumped a little when she felt his hand on her ass, but after a moment she continued to smooth the bedding into place. A sudden, sharp smack to her right ass cheek pulled a surprised cry from her lips. He had hit her quite hard, and she could feel the lingering heat of his handprint against her skin. She reached for one of the pillows and plumped it into position.

His hand crashed down on the other side, the force of the blow flattening her against the mattress. Suddenly he was on her, straddling her back with his legs. She was trapped beneath him — there was no way to continue her work. She lay there, unsure what to do. His hand found her ass again, this time smacking the end of the butt plug, pushing it deeper into her.

Hailey groaned at the pressure as pain radiated over her ass cheeks from his hard palm. He struck her again and again, covering every inch of her ass with strong, stinging blows. She began to pant. Tears seeped from the corners of her eyes. In spite of the pain and her position, or no—because of it—her cunt was sopping wet and aching to be filled.

All at once, his weight was lifted from her body. She heard him move behind her and she waited, silently willing him to flip her over and cover her body with his. She longed to be pinned down with his masculine weight as he plunged his hard cock inside her.

That didn't happen.

She lay still for several long moments, not sure what to do. Finally she dared to lift her head and twist it back to see what he was doing.

He was gone.

She bit back the deep sigh that welled inside her. She willed herself to get off the bed and back to work. Her ass was flaming, her cunt on a different kind of fire. It took supreme effort to focus on the task at hand. She re-straightened the bed and gathered the cleaning supplies. Moving slowly and carefully, she made her way back down the stairs to the supply closet. She listened for Master Ronan and surreptitiously glanced around, but he was nowhere in sight.

Biting back another sigh, she took the lightweight vacuum cleaner from the closet and hauled it back upstairs. She vacuumed the bedroom carpet. The hallway was hardwood, and she didn't see a speck of dirt on it. She vacuumed the stairs, balancing awkwardly in her hobble chain as she moved from one stair to the next until finally reaching the bottom floor.

Leaving the vacuum in the living room, she retrieved dusting supplies from closet and wiped down the shelves and furniture. Finally she vacuumed the beautifully patterned Oriental rug.

By the time she entered the kitchen, she was thirsty from her work. She wondered if she had permission to get some more of that delicious limeade she'd had the day before. She decided not to chance it—she would request permission later to take a drink during chores. Meanwhile she contented herself with a handful of tap water from the faucet.

She wiped down the countertop where they'd enjoyed the delicious sweet rolls and strong, hot coffee. She cleaned out the coffee pot and swept the floor, deciding she would mop last, after she washed and dried their few dishes.

She moved to the sink and turned on the water. As she was waiting for it to heat, she heard Master Ronan entering the kitchen, his bare feet swishing over the stone floor. She resisted her impulse to turn to him, instead picking up a coffee mug and squirting a dollop of dish soap into it.

She felt his hands on her shoulders, and the tickle of his breath beside her ear. "You're my property. I own you."

Hailey's knees threatened to buckle, his words thrilling her to her submissive core. "Yes, Sir," she breathed in agreement.

"I can do what I want to my property."

"Yes, Sir." A delicious tingle of fear shot through her longing.

She felt the sharp press of his teeth on the muscle where her shoulder met her neck. He growled as he lightly bit her. Lifting his head, he murmured, "Focus. Keep doing the dishes."

She realized the cup was hanging sideways in her hand, the water spilling over its side. She righted the cup and pushed a sponge into it. She blew out a breath as she tried to steady herself.

She heard him crouch down behind her. His hands were at her ankles, and he pulled open the hobble cuffs one at a time and then pushed the cuffs and chain away. Standing again behind her, he gripped her hips, pulling her lower half away from the sink so she was forced to bend at the waist to keep her position.

He tapped the inside of her ankle with a toe. "Stay like you are, but spread your legs shoulder-width apart. Keep them straight and stick out your ass," he commanded. His fingers were digging into the flesh just above her hips. He let go of one side and a moment later she felt the head of his cock between her legs.

She grunted as he rammed into her. Luckily she was slick with pent-up desire. The pressure in her ass increased as his cock competed inside her for space with the anal plug, the two phalluses separated only by a thin membrane. Grabbing both hips again, he thrust hard against her, pulled back and then thrust again.

"I" — thrust — "own" — thrust — "you," he grunted, each word punctuated with a brutal thrust that sent spirals of pure pleasure hurtling through Hailey's body.

She tried briefly to focus on the mug in her hand, but it was no use. She could barely see, much less concentrate on her duties. Something in the angle of his cock and the friction created by the dual phalluses inside her was creating sensations so powerful she was barely able to remain standing. She gripped the edge of the sink with her free hand and pressed her lips together to keep from screaming her pleasure.

Then she felt his fingers at her clit, and his touch sent a jolt of lightening through her frame. The cup fell from her fingers and clattered in the sink. His fingers moved over her swollen clit as he fucked her with ferocious perfection. It was too much. Though she'd been trained in orgasm control at The Compound, nothing had prepared her for an onslaught of this nature, and she found herself powerless in its grip.

"Please, Sir, oh please! May I come? I need to come. Oh god…"

"No. You may not." Again he punctuated his words with perfectly placed thrusts.

Tears of frustration sprang to Hailey's eyes, but she willed her body to obey her Master's cruel decree. She pressed her lips together to keep from begging again, but failed to stop the low moan of lust that rose deep in her throat.

Oh god, stop. Don't stop. Oh fuck, stop or I'll come. No! Master Ronan said no and that's the end of it. Don't come, don't come. You don't have permission. Wash the mug. Focus. Do your duty. Oh, oh, oh, oh…

He did something astonishing, a kind of swivel with his hips the left her completely without defense or the will to resist. It was no use. Her mouth opened and she heard herself wailing from a distance as a powerful orgasm ripped its way through her, obliterating conscious thought.

When she came to herself enough to focus, Master Ronan had pulled away from her. She was panting, her heart still galloping. She looked down to see that the handle of the mug had broken off when she'd dropped it. She lifted herself from her bent position and turned slowly and hesitantly to face her Master, the shame hot in her face.

He was naked, his cock still erect, his hands on his hips. "You came when I expressly forbid it." It wasn't a question.

There was less than no point in trying to deny what was so obvious. "Yes, Sir. I'm so sorry, Sir."

"I can see we have a lot of work to do. I only hope six months will be enough time." He flashed an evil grin. "What happens to girls who come without permission?"

Hailey's gut clenched. She could have whined that he'd set her an impossible task—that what he'd done was so amazing there was no way she could have resisted. She could try to appeal to his masculine ego, but she would not cheapen herself, or him, with such a ploy. She had begged for permission, and she had been refused. And that was that.

She lifted her chin and met his gaze, ready to take what she knew was coming to her. "They get punished, Sir."

Chapter 6

She was standing on her toes, her cunt poised just above the two-by-four between her legs. Her arms were bound behind her back with cotton bondage rope, securely tied at the wrists and elbows so she was forced to arch her back to keep her balance over the modified sawhorse.

Ronan kept his eyes on Hailey as his cell phone skittered and vibrated on the glass table. He didn't want to answer the damn phone, but it was the sixth time in the past hour his extremely annoying and persistent agent had called without leaving a message. He grabbed it and touched the screen.

"What?" he demanded brusquely.

"Ronan, babe. About time you picked up."

Ronan hated it when Armand called him babe, but he'd grown tired of pointing this out. "Did you forget? I'm on hiatus for the next six months. I told you not to bother me unless—"

"Unless it was an emergency. Yeah, I know, I know. I'm sorry to bug you, but you need to hear this. Too big to leave as a phone message or text." He paused, clearly waiting for a prompt. Ronan offered none.

"We got the gig, babe!" Armand shouted, the triumph ringing in his voice. "The Midnight Assassin trilogy! Filming is scheduled for next spring. They want you, man. No audition, no haggles, no nothin'. It's a done deal. All we need is your John Hancock and the wheels will turn. The money is fucking ridiculous, man. We're talking an astronomical payoff — front end and back end, share of the profits, executive producer rights, the whole shebang."

The thought of being locked into yet another series of mind-numbing action hero movies where the dialog consisted of grunted one-liners and the special effects superseded any attempt at plot did not gladden Ronan's heart — the money notwithstanding. This was definitely not what he had imagined for himself when he'd dreamed of making it as an actor.

"Dude! You there? Hello? Hello?"

Ronan forced himself to concentrate. The sooner he dealt with Armand, the sooner he could get back to what really mattered. "I'm here. Send me the stuff via email, okay? I'll have a look at it."

"That's *it*? You'll have a *look*? What the fuck, Ronan? This is the — "

"I said I'll have a look," Ronan interrupted, his jaws clenched. "If they want me that bad, they can wait a couple of damn days, right? You wouldn't want to seem too eager."

Armand laughed, though it sounded forced. "Right you are, Mr. Wolfe. Always thinkin'. Okay, okay. I'll send it. But do me a fucking favor, babe. *Read* the damn thing, okay?" He sighed histrionically into the phone. "Sheesh, sometimes I think your career matters more to *me* than to you."

A small shock went through Ronan's core, and he realized that was probably true. When, exactly, had he lost sight of his dreams? "Send the stuff. I'll read it and get back to you within a day or two."

Putting agents and action movies firmly out of his head, he refocused on the beautiful, naked woman he'd positioned over the punishment pony. He'd ordered a sawhorse from the home improvement warehouse, and then modified it so the thin edge of the central two-by-four plank was facing upward, perfect for fitting snuggly between labia. He'd carefully sanded and smoothed the wood to prevent splinters, though the beam retained its sharp angles, the edges perfect to punish that luscious cunt of hers.

She'd only been balanced over the beam for ten minutes, and he suspected those muscular, yoga-toned calves of hers would keep her on her toes a while longer. Her head was turned toward the ocean, her face a study of serene concentration.

He'd thought about exacting the punishment on the sand, but since he wasn't exactly sure how long she'd hold on, he'd set up the sawhorse beneath the veranda awning to protect her from the sun. He sat about ten feet away, angled so he could watch both her and the ocean at the same time as he sipped his limeade and idly stroked his cock.

Turning the cell phone off, he stood and moved toward Hailey. He stopped in front of her. "How're you doing?" He cupped her cheek with his palm. Her skin was smooth and warm.

She offered a tremulous smile. "My legs are getting tired, Sir, but I'm okay."

"You understand the nature of this punishment, right?"

"Yes, Sir."

"Explain it to me."

She swallowed and shifted slightly, still managing to hold herself above the narrow plank between her legs. "It's called predicament bondage, Sir. A matter of me choosing one erotic discomfort over the other. The task becomes increasingly difficult as my muscles begin to fatigue. As long as I can stay on my toes, I won't have to rest my body against the sharp edges of the wood. I control what happens."

Ronan withdrew his hand. "*I* control what happens, slave Hailey. At all times. What you will experience is a matter of cause and effect. Do you understand the difference?"

She paused a moment, and then nodded. "Yes, Sir."

He moved closer and slipped his fingers into the space between the wood and her cunt. He ran the tip of one finger along the edges of her outer labia. A small but discernable tremor moved through her frame, and her nipples hardened. Was it purely a physiological response to his touch, or was she responding specifically to him? Did it matter?

He pushed aside the questions and slid his finger gently into the tight opening at her center. She was wet, and the muscles of her cunt gripped his finger in a pleasing way. Her eyes opened slightly and her pupils dilated. Ronan's cock throbbed. He leaned closer. "You," he said in a low voice made hoarse by his lust, "are a greedy slut girl."

"Yes, Sir," she replied, a wash of color moving over her face and throat. "I'm sorry, Sir."

His finger still inside her, he laughed and shook his head. "Oh, no need to apologize. I like it. The thing is"—he withdrew his finger and brought it to his nose. He inhaled her delicate, spicy perfume—"you need to learn better control of your body. I love that you're responsive, but for some reason, despite all that fabulous training you had at The Compound, you don't seem to be able to control your impulses or your reactions all that well. In the two days you've been here, you've stolen two orgasms—one at your own hand, one on my cock, both times in direct contradiction to my dictates."

"Yes, Sir," she said faintly, tears suddenly welling in her dark blue eyes. Ronan felt almost guilty for making her cry, but he also understood her remorse was genuine, born out of a sincere desire to submit and obey. He owed it to her to punish her when it was called for. To do less would be to shirk his responsibility as her Master.

He stepped back and took a slow walk around the sawhorse. Her hands looked good — no circulation issues from the rope binding her arms and wrists. The butt plug protruded slightly between her ass cheeks, the edge of it pressed against the wood, though so far she was still managing to avoid direct contact to her labia. Her leg muscles were trembling ever so slightly from the strain of her position. It was only a matter of time before she was forced to lower herself to the wood.

"Permission to speak, Sir?"

"Yes."

"How long will I be on the horse, Sir?"

He'd worked with easily a dozen submissives while training at The Exchange, but even at its most intense, it had remained somehow academic — an exercise. At the end of it, he would shower, pack up and leave, shedding his Master persona along with the used towels as he left the club.

But this was different. This girl was the real thing, and she was his.

The realization was breathtaking.

"As long as it takes, slave girl. As long as it takes."

~*~

The sky was robin's egg blue and a cool sea breeze was gently blowing, but Hailey could feel the sweat trickling down her sides and gathering at the small of her back as her legs muscles strained. She'd already felt the bite of the wood as Master Ronan had adjusted the sawhorse just so beneath her when he'd first instructed her to climb over the horse. Both of them knew it was only a matter of time before she was forced to lower herself onto its hard, biting embrace. She tried to use her hands to lean back against the beam with her palms, and thus relieve some of the pressure in her calves, but with the way her arms were bound, she was unable to do it without fear of losing her balance altogether.

I'll lower myself for just a little while, she told herself, her legs now shaking with fatigue. *I'll rest my legs and then lift up again if it gets to be too much. He can't leave me on here forever.*

She glanced toward Ronan. He was watching her with the stillness of a beast of prey waiting to pounce. She slid her eyes from him, determined to handle her punishment without complaint. He was right—she lacked self-control, at least where he was concerned. She lacked discipline in this new environment. Though she'd thrilled to the training at The Compound, feeling, in a way, she'd come home for the first time in her life, it was the experience itself that had moved her, not the men who trained her.

Yet with Ronan—Master Ronan—it was different. It was real.

She lowered herself on wobbly legs until her feet were flat on the smooth flagstone. The relief was immediate in her calf muscles, but then she felt the intense pressure at her cunt, the sharp-edged beam digging deep between her inner labia and pinning her clit painfully between her pubic bone and the wood.

She tried rotating her hips back to shift the pressure from her cunt to her ass. The sudden thrust of the anal plug reminded her sharply of its presence. She gasped and jerked reflexively, nearly losing her balance on the beam. Her efforts to right herself were hampered by her bound arms behind her back. She shifted and wriggled without a shred of grace, the wood like a wedge of iron spreading her pussy lips wide as it drove into her cunt with unrelenting pressure.

Though her calf muscles still ached, she lifted herself once more to her toes, sighing with relief as the hard wood fell away from her tortured sex. She glanced again toward Ronan. He was naked, his large, erect cock fisted in his hand, his eyes hooded as he regarded her. Her predicament—her suffering—was exciting him. This wasn't merely a punishment for her, but a pleasure for him.

In another sort of person, one who wasn't hardwired for erotic pain and submission as Hailey was, this might have been an affront, an abuse. But for Hailey, it sent a pure jolt of deep, intense pleasure through her psyche. The realization that her erotic suffering excited him made it that much easier to bear, and made her all the more determined to endure her punishment with grace and courage.

This time her legs fatigued more quickly, and she was forced to lower herself once more into the hard, unyielding wood. She was so aroused at the sight of her Master stroking his shaft as he regarded her that the pain transmuted into pleasure. She rocked herself gently against the wood, letting it massage her swollen, distended clit. It felt good, the pain and the pleasure doing a lovely dance along her nerve endings.

All at once she realized what she was doing and she felt the heat flood her face. She was masturbating against the wood—engaging in precisely the behavior that had got her on this punishment pony in the first place. Chagrined, she rocked back to her ass, almost welcoming the sharp pain as the anal plug burrowed deeper inside her.

After a moment, she lifted herself to her toes, ignoring the cramp in her right calf. She glanced again at Ronan, praying he hadn't been aware of what she'd been doing.

He had risen to his feet and by the expression on his face, she understood he'd known exactly what she was doing. Her heart leaped into her throat. Was he angry?

He reached into a small duffel that sat on the table beside him and pulled something out. He walked toward her and stopped in front of the sawhorse. "I think," he said, holding up a pair of clover clamps, "you need some help with your focus. This is a punishment, not a pleasure ride, slut Hailey."

"Oh god," Hailey burst out in embarrassment. "I'm so sorry. I —"

"No," Master Ronan interrupted in a hard voice. "You do *not* have permission to speak."

She pressed her lips together and blinked back tears.

Ronan reached for her left nipple. He tugged it between thumb and forefinger until it was hard and fat in his grip. Pulling it taut, he opened one end of the clover clamps and positioned the grips on either side of her nipple. He released, and the pain was sharp and immediate.

Hailey kept her lips closed, drawing in a quick breath through her nostrils as she worked through the pain.

He did the same to the second nipple and this time a small moan of pain worked its way past her lips, though she managed to remain balanced on her toes. He lifted the chain between the clamps and touched the center links to her mouth. "Bite on it. Don't let it fall."

She took the chain between her teeth, the resulting increased tension adding to the intense pressure at her nipples. The initial sharp pinch had already subsided to a dull throb, and it wouldn't be long before her nipples numbed to something she could tolerate for an extended period—until the clamps were removed.

She focused once more on the sea, watching the waves tumble and roll like dolphins, glinting in silver and gold at the crests. *Serenity. Peace. Submission. Grace. Serenity. Peace. Submission. Grace. Serenity. Peace. Submission. Grace.* She could still feel the pain at her nipples and the intense pressure of the wood on which she had impaled herself, but instead of denying them, she reached inside her mind for them, and gathered them close to her heart. *I accept and embrace the pain. It is a part of me. My Master wishes this for me. It serves him and it serves me.*

The rapid tattoo of her heart slowly eased, her breathing slowing along with it. She could do this. She would suffer with grace and acceptance. It wasn't only her duty or her just dessert—it was her calling.

Then her calf cramped with the sudden viciousness of shark jaws slamming shut on their prey. Her feet hit the ground, causing her to thump down hard against the beam with all her weight. The wood jammed up between her labia and pinched them against her thighs. Miraculously, she managed to keep the clamp chain clenched in her teeth, though she couldn't stop the low, feral moan of agony.

She rocked back to ease the pressure, and felt the thrusting reproach of the anal plug inside her. She bit harder on the chain and lifted her chin, welcoming the distraction of the pressure at her breasts as she tried to shift into a less compromising position on the sawhorse. She attempted to rise again to her toes, but her muscles revolted, this time both calves cramping in refusal.

She sagged against the sawhorse, her entire body weight focused at her cunt, which pulsed with a burning sensation that left little room for arousal. To make matters worse, she realized her bladder was full. She tried leaning forward to ease the pressure, and nearly toppled over, her equilibrium off from the ropes binding her arms.

The wood was wedged hard against her clit. Each shift of her body only resulted in a different set of nerve endings firing in agony and pain. Cause and effect — her choice which body part to torture for how long in this ordeal of endurance — but Master Ronan was the one in control.

Tears were streaming down her cheeks. Snot was running down her face as well, sliding in an annoying ooze over her lips and chin, along with drool from her partially open mouth, the chain still clenched in her teeth. She stole another glance at her tormentor. He was watching her with hooded eyes, his expression inscrutable. He was seated at the table again, his body facing hers, his big, hard cock still fisted in his hand.

His eyes fixed on her, he began to move his hand slowly up and down his shaft, the movement incredibly erotic — or it would have been, if she hadn't been fighting to keep from screaming.

Her labia had numbed, but the pressure on her bladder was nearly intolerable. Hoping her legs muscles were sufficiently recovered, she lifted herself once more on her toes. A sudden stream of hot urine soaked the wood, splashing her legs as it puddled on the stone between her feet.

Hailey's mouth fell open with dismay as she realized what was happening, and the chain fell from her mouth. Ronan rose once more and headed toward her, his cock fat and red, his pleasure interrupted. Hailey was too mortified to protest, to explain, to do anything at all but gape at him as he approached.

He looked down at the pool of urine beneath the sawhorse. "My fault," he said. "I should have made you pee before you got on the horse." He shrugged. "No big deal. You can wash in the ocean once we're finished."

She waited, grateful for his calm assessment, desperate for him to let her down. He reached for her breasts, cupping each one in a hand, lifting them and letting them fall. "Look into my eyes," he commanded. "Keep your eyes open and focused on me."

He reached with both hands for the nipple clamps. A jab of fear stabbed Hailey's innards. "Focus on me," Master Ronan repeated, his voice like iron wrapped in silk. All at once, he released the clamps. The blood rushed into her nipples, bringing with it the searing pain of tortured nerve endings reawakened with a vengeance. Hailey felt faint from the pain, and her eyelids desperately wanted to flutter shut. She willed them to remain open, her focus on her Master's steady, calming gaze.

Mercifully, the pain quickly eased from poker hot needles to a steady, dull throb. She released the breath she hadn't realized she was holding, and drew another in its place. Master Ronan stroked her tender, aching nipples with feather-soft fingers. He cupped her breasts once more and then leaned down, taking one nipple tenderly between his lips.

Hailey leaned toward him as much as she could in her awkward, tethered position. If she could have melted away the rope and reduced the sawhorse to sawdust with a glance, she would have done so. She longed to reach for him, to pull him into her arms, to kiss his mouth, to somehow make him fall in love with her.

Instead she stood balanced on the beam, arms tightly bound behind her, all her weight painfully focused on the fulcrum of her impaled cunt. Master Ronan stepped back, removing the wet, sweet solace of his mouth from her breast. Hailey barely managed to bite back her sigh.

"Permission to speak?" she whispered hoarsely.

"Yes."

"Please, Sir. Can I get down? Is the punishment over?"

His countenance darkened and Hailey wished she could stuff the question back into her mouth. "It is not a slave's place to question her Master in this manner. You know better than that. I'm disappointed in you."

His words were like a slap in the face, and Hailey looked quickly down, tears of shame momentarily blinding her.

"You will remain on the horse until it pleases me to let you down," Master Ronan said, his voice hard. "Until I see you stop resisting. Until you embrace and welcome the pain you deserve. I will decide when it is over. I am the Master, sweetheart," he added, his voice suddenly gentle. She looked up to see he was smiling and her heart tugged with a sweet pain. "Or had you forgotten?"

It was as if a brake had pressed down on her pulse, slowing it, giving each beat a richer thud. His words, instead of sending her into a panic, had quite the opposite effect. They recalled her to herself. They made her realize she had been resisting the whole process every step of the way, biting, kicking and clawing her way through it. His words reminded her this punishment was not only punitive, but designed to teach. It was about growth, acceptance, and letting go.

"Forgive me, Sir. I forget myself. Thank you, Sir."

As Master Ronan stepped away, Hailey focused on her task with renewed resolve. She rocked forward and back on the unyielding wood, letting it wedge even more deeply between her labia and press like a fist against the anal plug. She no longer fought the pain or the pressure. She welcomed it with open arms. She let the pain grow until it was all there was, until it clawed through her cunt and ass and pawed deep in her belly like some kind of dark, snorting beast.

Through an act of sheer will, she hoisted herself onto the back of the beast, riding and twisting it until the alchemist in her somehow transformed the pain into pure, white-hot sensation. She could hear the ocean's waves crashing and receding in a steady percussive beat, the melody of her own soft moans and ragged breathing intertwining with the water's song.

With a last glance at her handsome Master, Hailey rode the galloping beast of erotic pain into the blinding silver light of the beckoning water. Together they sprinted away across the waves.

~*~

Watching the transformation in Hailey was like watching the sunrise over the water—first the shimmering promise of pink and palest gold as it struggled to break free of its confines, and then, all at once, the yellow orb bursting over the horizon in a brilliant fire of color.

Every last bit of resistance was burned away, and, though he knew she continued to suffer, the joy in her countenance told him she welcomed the pain. He was drawn to her, pulled from his seat by the magnetism of her sensual surrender. It was the first time since she'd been with him that he felt she gave of herself completely and without reservation. At the same time, he recognized she'd had all she could take, and he needed to act.

He moved quickly toward her, catching her as she slumped sideways. Holding her with one arm, he released the slipknots of rope from her wrists and upper arms. She sagged heavily against him as he lifted her carefully from the sawhorse and carried her to the yoga cabana. He lowered himself to the mat, Hailey still in his arms. She opened her eyes and smiled blearily at him. She mumbled something incoherent.

"Shh," Ronan said, smiling down at her. "Don't try to speak. Just rest. I'll take care of you."

She sighed and let her eyes flutter shut, her face a mask of blissful contentment. Ronan reached toward the basin he'd set in the cabana earlier, and pulled out the washcloth he'd left in the cool water. He squeezed out the cloth with one hand, cradling Hailey's shoulders in his other arm. He gently nudged her thighs apart and leaned over to examine her cunt. The labia were red and swollen, and some bruising already showed along her inner thighs. He dabbed gently between her legs with the damp cloth, drawing in his breath when he saw the red stain of blood on the cloth. He leaned closer to see the damage. There was only a small tear along the perineum, just a superficial scrape of skin.

He dipped the washcloth into the water once more, and carefully washed her a second time, relieved to see there was no more blood. Throughout it all she remained limp, a peaceful smile playing along the edges of her mouth.

Dropping the cloth into the basin, Ronan reached for the tube of salve. He squeezed some onto his fingertips and gently spread it on her inner thighs. He brushed it with feather-light strokes over her cunt. She shuddered and sighed as his fingers skimmed her clit, which was hard as a pebble. His cock nudged beneath her body in response, and he wondered if she could feel his erection against her ass.

He touched her clit again, running his index finger in a light, teasing circle around it. Her eyes opened, and she caught her lower lip in her small, white teeth. He looked deep into her eyes, dark as sapphires, as he moved his fingers in a sensual dance toward the slick heat of her entrance. He slid two fingers inside her, angling his hand so his palm pressed against her vulva. She groaned, and blinked rapidly, her eyes appearing to lose their focus.

"Look at me," Ronan ordered, his cock pulsing beneath her. "Keep your eyes open and on my face. I want you to come. You will ask me for permission at the time of orgasm. You will not look away from me, even during the climax."

"Yes, Sir," she whispered. "Oh, yes."

He increased the pressure of his palm as he stroked the silky soft, hot walls of her sex. Her pupils dilated and contracted, her mouth opening in a small, pink O as pain flitted over her features.

"Am I hurting you, slave Hailey?"

"A little, Sir, but it feels so good."

"Shall I stop?"

"No, Sir. Please, no."

He smiled, his cock hard as iron beneath her.

Her nipples, still marked from the clamps, looked like dark pink gumdrops, and he couldn't resist bending down to taste first one, and then the other. She moaned with each suck, and he increased the tempo of his fingers and palm as his hand danced against her cunt.

A tremor moved through her body, and he lifted his head to focus on her face. Her eyes locked onto his, and he stared into her soul as she began to tremble beneath his touch. "Please, Sir," she gasped. "I'm ready. Oh — oh, please, Sir, may I come, Sir?"

"Yes."

He quickened his movements, his hand flying over her sex, his fingers caught in the delicious, hot vise of her tight cunt as she shuddered, stiffened, and shuddered again in his grip. All the while her eyes remained fixed on his, the pupils large and black against the midnight blue of her irises, the lashes a thick fringe of dark, honey blond.

Unable to hold back a moment longer, Ronan leaned down and kissed her, crushing her soft lips with his, invading her mouth with his tongue as he gathered her close into his arms. He pulled her upright, positioning her so she straddled him, his cock trapped beneath her perfect ass. Lifting her, he lowered her until the tip of his cock pressed against the slick opening between her legs.

A spasm of pain moved over her face, her cunt still tender from the punishment it had endured on the sawhorse. Again, Ronan asked, "Am I hurting you, slave Hailey?"

Again, she replied, "A little, Sir," even as he felt the beckoning grip of her cunt muscles closing over the head of his cock.

Again, he asked, "Shall I stop?"

And once more, she replied, "No, Sir. Please, no."

Holding her by the hips, he pulled her down onto his shaft, groaning with ecstasy as her cunt sheathed his cock and clamped tight around it. He wanted to make it last, but each delicious thrust was an explosion of pure sensual perfection. He tried to resist for a minute or two, but she had begun to tremble once more, a series of sweet, breathy sighs stoking his senses as her cunt milked his shaft in a tight, wet grip. His heartbeat was a jackhammer, breaking up things inside him he hadn't realized were there. Unable to hold back anymore, he let go, spurting in a series of hard, fast bursts. He held her tight as he climaxed, burying his face in her neck as he experienced one of the most powerful orgasms of his life.

When he finally lifted his head, he realized with a shock that his cheeks were wet. Hailey was regarding him with a quizzical, tender expression. "Are you okay, Sir?" she asked softly. She lifted a finger, brushing away a tear.

He swallowed hard and nodded brusquely to hide his embarrassment and confusion. "Yes. Yes, of course. I'm fine." Still holding her, he hoisted himself to his feet. He set her carefully down. "How about you? You okay?"

She smiled like an angel. "Yes, Sir. I feel *amazing.* Purified. Light as air." She covered her bare mons with a hand and ducked her head demurely. "And a little sore, I'll admit."

He smiled back. "How about a dip in the ocean before lunch? Salt water is good for sore cunts."

"You think?" she said, eyebrows arched with skepticism.

Ronan laughed. "Only one way to find out. I'll race you down."

"Deal!" She sprinted suddenly away, dashing from the veranda to the sand before he could move. Astonished, he watched her lithe figure as she hurtled toward the water.

Finally getting himself into gear, he took off after her with a laugh, not stopping until he'd caught her again. Wrapping her in his arms, he pulled her close, lifting her high as the waves crashed over them in a cold, salty spray.

Chapter 7

"Tell me it isn't true!" George said when Ronan picked up his call.

"Well, hello to you, too," Ronan laughed. "What? What isn't true?"

"I just read in *Us Magazine* that you and Scarlett Johansson have broken up. And speculations are rising about Blake Lively's baby bump. Is it yours? Are you going to make an honest woman of her?"

"What the fuck?" Ronan sputtered. "Scarlett and I did a movie, that was it, period. I never even met Blake Lively."

"That's not what *The Star* says, kiddo." George began to laugh, his big, hearty guffaw so loud Ronan had to hold the phone away from his ear.

"Sorry," Ronan muttered, chagrined. "You know I hate all that gossip shit. I should have realized you were kidding."

"Ya think?" George continued to chuckle.

"So, what's up, George?"

"What's up? It's been two weeks since I delivered that gorgeous slave girl to your doorstep, and I haven't heard a peep out of you. How's it going?"

Ronan looked through the open veranda doors into the living room, where the housekeeper was busy waxing the floor. Though she probably couldn't hear him, Ronan stood and walked down the steps to the sand for more privacy. "It's going spectacularly well, actually. She's well-trained, but with room for improvement. Every day is a new adventure. We're both learning all the time. She's everything I was hoping for and more. I feel so...I don't know what the word is."

"Happy?" George suggested.

Ronan laughed. "Yeah. I guess that would cover it. Except, well...the damn staff gets in the way. They're here all the time—cooking, cleaning, gardening, what have you. This place is too fucking much work to maintain."

"The staff gets in the way? How do you mean?"

"I mean I have to hide her up in the dungeon when they're working. Obviously, I can't have a naked slave girl parading around when they're here. Confidentiality agreement or no, I doubt they could keep their mouths shut about *that*."

"So put some clothes on her. Introduce her as your girlfriend."

"My *girlfriend*?"

"It's not a dirty word, my friend. People have them all the time. In fact, I just read in the *National Enquirer* that you have three different girlfriends, none of whom know about the other. There's Scarlett, of course. And then there's Blake and Penelope—"

Ronan laughed. "Okay, okay. Yeah. That's not a bad idea. Though she's not my girlfriend, of course."

"Of course," George echoed.

"I don't do that whole girlfriend thing. You know that. This is strictly a Master-slave thing. A contract."

"I'm not arguing with you."

Ronan started to add more, but realized he sounded defensive, and snapped his mouth closed. George continued, "So, when do I get to see the lovely slave Hailey again? I took quite a shine to her, you know."

"Why don't you come over for dinner tonight?"

"I have a better idea. It's one of the reasons I called. I managed to get reservations at *Gerard's*. The reservation waiting list is a mile long, but I know someone who knows someone." He laughed. "Seriously, though. I've been wanting to check it out forever, and it would give Hailey a kick, I bet. Small town girl and all."

"You know I can't go to a restaurant in LA without it turning into a fucking three-ring circus."

"Relax. I managed to get us one of the private rooms. There's a back entrance and everything. Totally incognito and extremely discreet. They're used to all that hush-hush-avoid-the-paparazzi-hoo-hah. No one will even know we're there. Come on. You can't hide out on your Malibu compound forever."

"Hailey has nothing suitable to wear. She brought clothing, but it's all hippie stuff. Jeans, cotton skirts, stuff like that. She would feel out of place."

"So buy her a dress."

"You know I can't go out shopping without being mobbed," Ronan retorted with more vehemence than he'd intended. It wasn't George's fault that his latest action-packed movie posters were plastered on billboards and the sides of buses from one side of the city to the other.

Taking this hiatus after coming off a grueling three-year schedule of non-stop filming was the best decision he'd ever made. But when it was over, then what? As his agent liked to point out—if you don't keep your face in front of them, they'll just move on to the next new thing. But would that be so bad?

He still hadn't committed to the deal Armand was so eager for him to take, and just the thought of signing his life away for another three movies filled him with dread. How he missed the simpler days when he had worked as a carpenter, making custom furniture in his garage. When had his life become so circumscribed? When had he stopped having fun?

"Okay, so *I'll* take her to find a dress," George volunteered. "Anything else you want while we're out? You got all the whips and toys you need?"

The question gave Ronan a deliciously diabolical idea, and he realized an evening out could present some intriguing possibilities. "You say the room at the restaurant is totally private?"

"Not even near the main dining room. So, it's a go?"

"Yeah. It's a go. And yes—there are a few things I'd like you to pick up…"

~*~

Hailey had been dozing on her mattress when Master Ronan entered the small room earlier that afternoon. She was dreaming, and in the dream, she was back in her cottage in Vermont, the crisp cool air blowing through the open window of her small bedroom, carrying the scent of honeysuckle and freshly mown hay. She could hear the comforting burble of the creek behind the house. In her dream, Ronan was still Master Ronan, but he was also her husband, and he didn't hide her away when other people were in the house, but met them with his arm around her shoulders, and his ring on her finger. She didn't sleep alone in a tiny room off a dungeon, but in his arms in their bed. It was a good dream.

When Ronan had wakened her, it had taken several disorienting seconds before she returned to the reality of her present situation. She'd nearly embarrassed herself by reaching for him and giving him a kiss.

She had been excited, though, when he'd told her of their plans for the evening. While she had loved every moment as Master Ronan's slave, she hadn't left his home since her arrival, and she'd seen nothing of California. Though she would rather have been sitting beside Ronan as they drove along the Pacific Highway toward LA, it was good to see George. She'd only known him a short while, but it was like seeing an old friend.

The traffic slowed to a crawl as they reached the outskirts of LA, and there was a gray haze on the horizon, smudging the perfect blue of the sky. George kept up a running commentary as he drove about what they were seeing, and which famous actor lived where, though it meant little to Hailey.

Finally they pulled to a stop in front of an expensive-looking boutique on Rodeo Drive. Two valets rushed over to open their doors. Several men with cameras around their necks lifted their heads and eyed Hailey critically as they walked toward the entrance. George put his arm around her and said, "Ignore them. Vultures looking for prey."

He rang a doorbell at the front of the door, and a moment later they were buzzed inside. The whole place was white—white walls, white wood floors, white mannequins that looked like marble statues. There didn't seem to be all that many racks of clothing, but what there was appeared to be arranged by color.

A tall, impossibly thin young woman with her hair pulled back in a severe bun and more makeup than Hailey wore in a year approached them. She was dressed in a long silk jacket and matching very short skirt, six-inch platform shoes on her feet. She eyed Hailey with one eyebrow cocked disapprovingly.

"May I help you?" Her tone indicated she doubted such a thing was possible.

George spoke up. "My esteemed companion, Princess Hailey Grimaldi of Monaco, would like an outfit suitable for *Gerard's*. Dress, shoes, the whole shebang. Money, naturally, is not an issue."

Hailey suppressed a grin as the woman's demeanor underwent a complete one-eighty, and she actually bobbed an awkward curtsey in Hailey's direction. "Of course, Sir. Right this way, Your Majesty."

"I'll just wait over here, Princess," George said, pointing to a leather and chrome contraption that looked something like a chair. "You can model for me."

The saleswoman brought Hailey to a huge private dressing room. "My name's Brittany. Can I get you a glass of wine? Some Perrier?"

"No, thanks. I'm good."

"I'll just bring in some things for you to try. I have several things in mind that would be perfect for you. You're what, a size six?"

"Yes."

The woman nodded happily. "I can always tell. Shoe a size seven and a half?" Again Hailey agreed. "We just got in some Christian Louboutins that would look fab on you," Brittany gushed. "I'll be right back, okay?"

Hailey nodded and smiled. "Thanks."

Once alone, she glanced around the room, all four walls of which were covered with mirrors. The lighting was muted, and gave Hailey's skin a rosy glow. Brittany returned a moment later with an armload of dresses. Another woman was behind her balancing six shoeboxes in her arms.

"If you'll just disrobe, Your Highness," Brittany said, hanging a dozen dresses on a rack.

"Oh." Hailey felt herself blushing. "I'll just try them on alone, if you don't mind." Brittany looked confused. She glanced at the other woman, who was opening the shoeboxes and placing them in a neat row beneath the dresses. "I'm a little shy," Hailey lied.

"Of course." Brittany nodded her understanding, and she and the other woman glided out of the room, closing the door softly behind them.

Hailey took off her tank top, slipped out of her sandals and removed her cotton skirt. She wore nothing beneath the garments, and had removed the slave collar per Master Ronan's dictate before leaving his house. She touched her bare throat as she regarded herself in the mirror. The skin there was paler than elsewhere, a reminder of her lack. Welts, both new and faded, striped her back, ass and thighs, and there were faint bruises on her ass from a spanking delivered the night before. It was these marks, rather than any shyness, that kept Hailey from stripping in front of the saleswomen.

But what would probably horrify the two of them brought a broad smile to Hailey's face, and she hugged herself happily at the memory the delicious skin-on-skin spanking. They had been walking together along the beach, hand in hand, just like a real couple, when Master Ronan had pulled her down to the sand and ordered her to drape herself over his legs. He'd given her a delicious, hard spanking, the kind that cleanses the soul and sends the spirit soaring. Afterward he'd let her suck his beautiful cock and she'd happily swallowed every salty-sweet drop.

She turned to the dresses Brittany had chosen and tried them on, finally settling on a dress of champagne satin with lace appliqués and tiny colored stones embroidered along the edges and at the waist. There were matching shoes that fit perfectly, and she chose these as well. There were no price tags on anything, and she could only imagine what an outfit like this must cost, but thought about the saying, "If you have to ask..."

Recalling George's request that she model her selection for him, she went out of the dressing room, walking carefully on the high heels to assure her movements were graceful.

George, who had been doing something on his cell phone, looked up as she approached and gave a low, appreciative whistle. "My, my, my, but don't you look lovely, Your Majesty. You ever considered a career in pictures?" He winked as Brittany and the other woman rushed over.

"It's perfect," Brittany enthused. "Maybe just a little tuck here at the waist." She pinched a bit of fabric and George nodded his agreement. "We have a seamstress in back who can do it in fifteen minutes, tops."

"Fine, fine," George said, getting to his feet. "We'll take it. The shoes too. Throw in a pair of stockings while you're at it. We have another stop to make, and then we'll be back to pick it up, okay?"

Hailey changed back into her own clothes, and they left the boutique, moving through the still-idling paparazzi waiting to catch a glimpse of the rich and famous buying their clothes. They drove along the wide, traffic-clogged boulevards, Hailey asked, "Where are we going now?"

He turned toward her with a wolfish grin. "To a little BDSM shop Ronan likes. There are a couple of things he wants you to pick up for tonight's excursion." One hand on the wheel, he reached into his pants pocket and pulled out a folded piece of paper, which he handed to Hailey.

She opened it and read:

Venus Butterfly

Vibrating Anal Beads

"Oh," Hailey said, her heart skipping a beat. "He wants *me* to pick these out?"

George, eyes on the road, nodded, his mouth curving into a grin. "Yep. Parking's a bitch where we're going. If I can't find a spot, I'll try to wait outside the shop while you run in. Just ask one of the helpful salespeople to show you around. You'll love it in there. A candy store for fetishists." He reached into his pocket again, pulling out some crisply folded bills. He held out the money, his eyes still on the road. "Here's some cash for the purchase."

Hailey accepted the money, not knowing what else to do. She realized she was holding five one-hundred-dollar bills. "That seems like an awful lot for just those two things."

"Oh, yeah. Ronan threw in a couple of hundred extra, in case something else catches your eye."

Hailey slipped the list and the money into the small purse she'd brought along on the outing. George put on his turn signal and began easing the car into the right lane. "Okay, it's just up here. I'll pull up front. If I can't wait, I'll circle around and come back."

Hailey climbed out of the car and stared up at the storefront. She'd expected to see a mannequin in the window wearing leather fetish gear and a ball gag, or something equally garish. Instead, the place was a nondescript building of beige stucco with a green awning over the glass front door. The words *Mistress Jayne's House of Payne* was painted in gold lettering at eye level. As with the clothing boutique, Hailey had to ring a doorbell to gain access. A mature woman in a tailored black silk pantsuit peered through the glass and then opened the door.

"Welcome," she said in a deep, smoky voice as she gestured Hailey inside. "What can I do for you today?"

Hailey swallowed, feeling a little ridiculous. Here she was, a fully trained BDSM sex slave, and she felt embarrassed to ask for the items on the list. "I'll just look around, thanks."

"Absolutely. Take your time." The woman melted away as Hailey stepped into the space. The long, rectangular room was filled from floor to ceiling with more BDSM paraphernalia and gear than Hailey had ever seen in one place, even the fully equipped dungeons at The Compound. There were several other people milling around, some in pairs, some by themselves.

Hailey moved past the racks of fetish wear and the BDSM furniture and cages. At the back of the store she found what she was looking for—a large display of every conceivable kind of dildo and vibrator. She eyed the wares for a while until she saw the grouping of vibrating anal toys. Master Ronan had been working with her on anal training, and while she was getting more comfortable with his attention in that area, she didn't love it. He had told her when she stopped resisting—when she truly gave of herself in that regard—the love would naturally follow, but so far that had yet to happen.

She shuddered as she eyed strings of anal beads as big as baseballs, wondering how anyone could accommodate something like that, and moved past the ping pong-sized beads, settling finally on a set of beads the size of large marbles. They came with a remote control and, the package informed her with exclamation points, batteries were included.

Next she scanned the area, looking for the Venus Butterfly. She had seen the clit stimulator used on one of her fellow trainees at The Compound who had trouble achieving orgasm. Hailey had certainly never had a problem achieving orgasm with Master Ronan—quite the contrary. Still, he wanted her to buy it, so buy it she would.

Her eyes moved past vibrators of all shapes and sizes with myriad attachments. Finally she saw the packaged item she was looking for. The butterfly-shaped stimulator was wrapped in clear plastic, and made from soft, purple rubber.

Items in hand, Hailey started to head toward the cashier's counter at the back of the store, but she was distracted by a heavyset man who was holding the arm of an equally heavyset woman. He was running a kind of wand, its head made from a globe of glass, along the woman's arm. As it made contact, it flashed and sparkled like it was filled with lightning, and made a crackling sound.

The woman shivered and laughed. "Oh, do it again! Do it again!"

"Like what you see?"

George's voice by her ear startled Hailey, and she whirled to face him. "Oh! I thought you were waiting —"

"Miracle of miracle's, I found a spot." The woman tittered again, and George, following Hailey's gaze, said, "That's a violet wand. Ever have one used on you?"

Hailey shook her head, unable to tear her eyes away from the demonstration. The man had put a different head on the wand, this one a kind of roller with tiny spikes on it. Sparks of purple and silver light flashed as he rolled it along the woman's inner arm. This time she squealed.

George chuckled. "I think we've found the toy for you, slave Hailey." He strode toward the couple and turned back to Hailey. "Come over here. I want you to try this out for yourself."

George was already introducing himself to the couple as Hailey approached. "And this is slave Hailey. She's never experienced the shocking pleasure of a violet wand."

"Oh," the woman enthused. "You'll love it, honey. We have three sets already at home. It feels *incredible*, especially on freshly whipped skin."

"Want to try it out?" George asked.

Hailey swallowed nervously but nodded, her body tingling with anticipation. The man, who introduced himself as Master Franklin, removed the spiked head and replaced it with a glass head shaped like a mushroom. He took Hailey's wrist gently in his large hand and extended her arm. She tensed as he brought the wand close to her skin. Tiny bolts of lightening flew from the wand, and a fizzing sensation tickled along her skin, just this side of pain.

"Oh," Hailey said softly, though she hadn't meant to speak.

The man laughed. "There's that look," he said with a knowing grin. "I call it the greedy slave girl look. She wants it. She wants it bad."

Hailey, embarrassed, pulled her wrist away. George put a comforting arm around her shoulders. "She wants it good, you mean," he said with a smile. "Which kit would you recommend for beginners?"

Ten minutes later they were in the car. They stopped at the clothing boutique, and this time Hailey waited while George went in and retrieved her new outfit, which he lay out on the backseat in its garment bag, along with a bag containing her new shoes and several pairs of stockings. Finally they escaped the snarl of traffic and Hailey breathed a sigh of relief as they headed back to Malibu.

She couldn't wait to get home.

Chapter 8

The three of them sat around a circular table covered in a snowy linen tablecloth and set with gold plates and crystal, Hailey seated between the two men. She looked radiant. Her lovely dark blue eyes sparkled in the candlelight of the sumptuous private dining room to which they'd been whisked upon arrival at the trendy restaurant.

The attentive waiter had taken his leave, after uncorking and pouring a very fine wine for them and presenting his dissertation on the night's special menu. Though the private room was elegant and comfortable, Ronan felt a sudden jab of regret that they had to hide out in a back room like fugitives.

He quickly shook the regret away, all too aware what the cost of letting the rabid public see him with someone new would be. It wasn't that he never went out in public. Though he hated the attention, he understood it was a part of his job. But to expose Hailey to the insanity was beyond unfair—it was criminal. No. Better to focus on the pleasures of the evening—the excellent food, the luxurious atmosphere, and his deliciously evil plans.

As George regaled Hailey with an amusing tale from a BDSM party at the club, Ronan took out the velvet toy pouch and set it casually on the table beside Hailey's plate. She looked from the bag containing the anal beads, the butterfly and a small tube of lubricant to meet Ronan's gaze. He touched her arm with a single finger. Hailey instantly shifted her gaze from George to Ronan.

"It's time," Ronan said in a soft voice. "Use the private bathroom. Insert the items and bring me the remotes."

Hailey bit her lower lip, but closed her hand over the pouch. Meeting Ronan's eye, she nodded. "Yes, Sir." Both men stood as Hailey left the table. She moved gracefully toward the small powder room just off the private dining area, her small, shapely ass swaying in the sheer fabric of her new gown.

After a discreet knock, the waiter reentered, a second waiter behind him, both of them carrying trays of food. The second waiter set his tray on the marble serving counter set against one wall and discreetly melted away. Their waiter took his time arranging various platters on the table and refilling the wine glasses.

Finally, with an obsequious smile, he said, "And if there's anything else—"

"Thanks, no," Ronan said abruptly, eager for him to be gone before Hailey returned. "We're good for now. In fact, we need about twenty minutes without any interruption. Is that a problem?"

"No, Sir. No problem at all. Just ring that bell if you need anything before that, anything at all, Sir." He nodded toward the doorbell that had been installed in the wall just behind Ronan's chair and then backed silently from the room, his hands held out in a supplicating gesture that annoyed Ronan. Something about the waiter didn't sit right with him.

"I don't trust that guy," he said to George.

George nodded. "I know what you mean. He's got shifty eyes. But the staff here signs confidentiality agreements and nobody's even allowed to carry a cell phone while they're working. If he wants to keep his job, he'll keep his mouth shut, no matter what. Just the same, I think I noticed a lock on the door. Shall I?"

Ronan nodded. "Good idea. Though Hailey doesn't need to know that."

"You're such a sadist, Wolfe."

"Takes one to know one."

George laughed. "Indeed."

Just as George returned from locking the door, Hailey reappeared, a shy smile on her face. The way the light shone in the room, she seemed to be outlined in gold, and her nipples were just visible, poking against the front of her dress. Ronan's cock stiffened as he watched her approach the table.

She placed the empty pouch on the table by Ronan's plate, along with the remote controls. She started to sit down, but Ronan stopped her. "I want you under the table, slave girl. I have need of your services." He pointed toward his lap. Hailey glanced at George, her cheeks turning pink, but after a moment she caught herself, and nodded.

Lowering to her knees, she slipped obediently beneath the table. She positioned herself between Ronan's legs and reached for his belt. He scooted forward on his chair to assist her as she unzipped his fly. Her long, cool fingers wrapped tantalizingly around his shaft as she pulled it from the flap at the front of his underwear. He could barely suppress the groan of pleasure as her mouth closed over the head of his cock and slid down, taking in his length.

Suddenly remembering the toys, Ronan reached for the two remotes. He flicked each one to its lowest setting. The faint sound of the toys coming to life whirred beneath the table. George grinned and mouthed, *You lucky bastard.* As Hailey's soft, wet tongue slid tantalizing up and down his shaft, Ronan had to agree.

With a wink and a grin, George began to talk, updating Ronan on the latest gossip at the club. They'd scened together with women at the club, so he knew George was comfortable with what was happening under the table. Ronan listened with half an ear to George's stories, his focus increasingly on what was happening to his cock.

He flicked the remotes up a notch, and Hailey gasped against his shaft, but she kept her focus admirably. It wasn't long before he felt the tightening in his balls that signaled his fast-approaching orgasm.

He reached under the table and gripped a handful of Hailey's luxuriant hair in one hand, cupping the other against the back of her neck as he spurted deep into her throat.

When he opened his eyes, George was regarding him with an amused expression. "Feel better?"

Ronan barked a laugh. "Oh, yeah." He started to offer George a turn, but somehow the words stuck in his throat. He realized with a small shock that he didn't want to share Hailey. Somehow in the past couple of weeks she'd become more than just a highly trained slave for hire. Though he knew it was temporary, she was *his*, damn it, and he didn't want to share.

As if reading his thoughts and intuiting his feelings, his old friend preemptively let him off the hook. "I had a great session today at the club. That girl wore me out. So I guess that just leaves slave Hailey down under the table still in need of release." He lifted his eyebrows. "That's something I would dearly love to see."

Ronan nodded eagerly, more than happy to accept this tacit compromise. Lifting the tablecloth, he looked under the table. Hailey was crouched on her knees, the anal balls and butterfly vibrating between her legs. "Clean me up," Ronan ordered. "Then sit back down at the table. George and I want to watch you come."

He dropped the cloth and sat back, sighing happily as Hailey licked his balls and shaft, and then tucked him back into his underwear, zipped his trousers and buckled his belt. Her blond head appeared, and then the rest of her as she lifted herself to her seat between the two men.

Ronan stopped her with a hand on her arm. "Lift your dress before you sit. Bare skin on the seat," he commanded quietly. Hailey's color was high, her eyes bright. Ronan wondered how close to orgasm she was from the vibrating toys doing their job between her legs, and how long she could hold out. It would be fun to find out.

She lifted the skirt of her dress and set herself daintily on the edge of the velvet seat, the heavy linen folds of the tablecloth hiding her lower half from view. Ronan rested his hand lightly on his slave girl's thigh. She shivered ever so slightly at his touch, which aroused the Dom in him still further. He slid his hand between her legs. Her bare cunt radiated heat, and he could feel the steady vibrating thrum of the butterfly at her clit.

Looking at George, Ronan said casually, "So, tell me about the new sub girl you've been working with at the club. How's that going?"

"Ah!" George said enthusiastically, his eyes fixed firmly on Hailey, "it's going great. She's into blood play, and I've been expanding my horizons in that arena. I've been studying with Master Leonard, the club's expert in needle and knife play. Did you ever work with him?"

"That's an area I have yet to explore." Ronan glanced toward Hailey. "Maybe that's something we should look into. What do you think, Hailey?"

He watched the war of emotions moving over her face—fear of needles, squeamishness at the thought of seeing her own blood battling with her masochistic need for erotic suffering and the desire to obey. For the moment, at least, obedience won, and she said in a low, serious voice, "As you wish, Sir. It's for you to decide."

"Yes," he agreed with a nod. "When the time comes, I will decide."

He flicked both remotes up a notch, and the small but unmistakable sound of the vibrating beads and butterfly hummed like little bees beneath the table. Hailey caught her breath, her body stiffening beside him. He lifted his glass of wine and took a long sip. "So, you were saying…" he said to George, barely able to contain his grin.

George said something poetic about the beauty of the flash of silver against the dark pink of the woman's nipple, and then the sudden blossom of a bright red droplet of blood at its tip. His words were clearly chosen for Hailey's benefit, if benefit was the right word.

George's gaze was fixed on Hailey as he said, "Have you ever thought about piercing slave Hailey's nipples?"

"She isn't mine," Ronan replied. "I haven't the right." Though the declaration came from his own mouth, he was surprised how deep the words cut. Hailey didn't appear to have heard their conversation. Her cheeks were flushed, her eyes glassy, her body trembling. Ronan turned the toys to their highest vibration.

Hailey's mouth fell open, a sheen of perspiration appearing on her upper lip. Ronan could smell the intoxicating siren's scent of her arousal, and feel the answering tug of his cock. Unable to resist, he reached a hand into the low neckline of her dress, seeking her erect nipple with his fingertips.

As he rolled the hard nubbin between his fingers, Hailey shuddered, a soft, sensual moan escaping her lips. Ronan had a sudden, vivid image of lifting her from the chair and pressing her against the table. He wanted to yank her dress to her waist, position himself between her spread knees and thrust himself into her wet heat. It was all he could do to remain seated.

"Christ, you are a lucky man," George murmured, and Ronan realized with a start he'd forgotten where they were, or who was watching. He glanced at his watch, and saw they were only minutes away from the serving of the main course.

"Do it, slave girl," Ronan commanded in a low, urgent voice, as he ratcheted the remotes to their highest settings. "Come for me. Come for George. Show us what a good, obedient slut you are."

"Oh, oh. Oooo, Sir. Yes, Sir, thank you, Sir," Hailey moaned. Her hands fluttered up to her chest and then clutched into fists as she shook on her seat. Her breathy moans and sighs wove into an erotic melody just above the hum of the vibrators moving in tandem against and inside her body.

There was a light knock at the door, just as Hailey stiffened in an orgasm that held her frozen for several intense beats. "A moment," George called.

Ronan flicked off the remotes as George rose and went to unlock the door. Hailey slumped back in her seat, her chest heaving, her mouth slack. A small series of aftershocks shuddered through her frame. George stood waiting, his hand on the doorknob.

"Compose yourself," Ronan said quietly to his slave girl, who at once sat at attention, though her cheeks and throat were rosy with a post-orgasmic flush, her hair tousled about her face.

At a nod from Ronan, George unlocked the door and returned to his seat. "Come in," Ronan called out. As the waiter stepped into the room, his shifty eyes flickered hungrily over Hailey, seeming to linger on her luscious cleavage. Ronan resisted the urge to snap at him to put his eyes back into his head. Instead, he put his hand over Hailey's and squeezed it with real affection. Leaning close, he murmured, "You were spectacular." She rewarded him with a dazzling smile.

The waiter busied himself at the sidebar, setting down trays and maneuvering dishes. Hailey's expression had once more smoothed to a serene mask. She smiled shyly at Ronan, who smiled back.

Once the waiter had gone again, Ronan excused Hailey from the table to remove the toys and clean herself up before the meal. While she was in the bathroom, George said quietly, "I have to admit, Ronan, I never thought I'd see the day."

"What?" Ronan asked. "What are you talking about?"

"You know what I'm talking about it."

"No, I don't," Ronan lied. Was it that obvious?

"You're falling for her. It's written all over your face."

Ronan shrugged, trying to keep his tone light. "Nah. I mean, don't get me wrong — she's great. The best. You did a hell of a job finding her, George. But falling?" He shrugged again, aware George wasn't buying his story, though he stuck to it. "You know me better than that. Ronan Wolfe never falls. I'm impervious. Just ask *People Magazine*." He managed a grin.

"Yeah, okay. Play it that way if you want."

Mercifully, George let it drop as Hailey returned to the table. Ronan realized he was starving, and turned his focus to the food. Everything was delicious, the menu especially chosen for them by Gerard himself, who appeared midway through the meal in his crisp white chef uniform to inquire if they were enjoying the repast, and if there was anything else they needed, anything at all. Ronan assured the man, famous in his own right, that the food and the service were excellent.

The three of them talked amiably and easily as they ate, and Ronan was glad Hailey felt comfortable and free enough to contribute to the conversation. She was bright, funny and perceptive. When asked, she entertained them with stories about her training at The Compound, which she infused with humility and grace, even while making them laugh. The rest of the evening passed pleasantly, and they managed to consume two bottles of wine with their meal. They all agreed they were too full for dessert, though they did enjoy some espresso and fresh berries with vanilla cream.

"This was a great idea," Ronan said to George as the three of them prepared to leave. "Thanks for getting us out."

"My pleasure," George said warmly, his eyes twinkling as he added, "And thank you for your graceful submission, Hailey, dear. You were breathtaking, as always."

Hailey blushed prettily and smiled at the floor. Ronan pressed the bell to summon the waiter. "Can you have my car ready out back, please?" He had already arranged to cover the dinner bill beforehand, not wanting George to have the chance to pay. He handed the valet ticket to the young man, who took it with a nod and disappeared.

Ronan put his arm around Hailey as they walked down the narrow hallway toward the outside exit. As they stepped into the night, a sudden blinding rush of lights flashed. A swell of people swarmed toward them like human locusts, buzzing with menacing intent.

"It's Wolfe! That's Ronan Wolfe!"

"See, I told you the tip was good."

"Hurry! Ronan! Over here! Look over here!"

More lights flashed as the crowd closed in around them like piranhas on the scent of blood. Hailey shrank against Ronan and turned her face from the lights.

"What the fuck?" Ronan swore, instinctively drawing Hailey closer.

"Ronan, who's the knockout girl? Do we know her?"

"Hey, sweetheart! Look this way! Smile for the camera, babe!"

Hailey stared with dazed, frightened eyes toward the oncoming mob waving cell phones and cameras like pitchforks and brooms. Ronan dropped his arm from Hailey's shoulders and pushed her toward George, who swept her from the fray as Ronan turned to face the paparazzi. He had learned the hard way that if you showed even the slightest hint of irritation at having cameras and microphones shoved into your face at any time of the day or night, for any reason whatsoever, you would be vilified in the gossip rags as an arrogant prick who didn't appreciate his fans. The backlash that invariably resulted would affect everyone with you. Damn it, he should have followed his first instincts and kept Hailey home, safe and sound. Instead all he could do now was damage control. "I'm just out with some old friends," he said with a forced smile, hoping he'd managed to keep the murderous fury from his tone.

"Get her into the car," Ronan called as a section of the paparazzi broke away from him to cluster around Hailey and George. They were peppered with questions as the cameras clicked relentlessly. Though it seemed like an hour, in reality only seconds passed before George managed to slide with Hailey into the backseat.

Thrusting a tip into the valet's open hand, Ronan jumped into the driver's seat, rage pulsing in his head like a hammer. Forcing himself to call out a good night to his attackers, Ronan gunned the engine and made his getaway.

~*~

"It's okay, really. I'm fine, I promise."

The three of them were sitting in Ronan's study, a room Hailey had never spent much time in before. Ronan, who had barely spoken during the drive from the restaurant, still looked grim-faced as he stared down into his brandy snifter. He'd already apologized a dozen times for the paparazzi invasion, and though it had been rather shocking while it was occurring—all the flashing lights and peering faces waving cameras and cell phones as they shouted—it had happened so quickly Hailey had barely had time to register what was going on.

"I'm sorry it got out somehow that we were there, but really, other than an annoyance, there's no real harm done," George added. "Armand will be thrilled. You know what he says—any press is good press. Now the blogs can go wild with speculation about Ronan Wolfe's mystery girl."

Though he still didn't look too happy, Ronan nodded and forced a smile. "I guess. As long as you're sure you're all right, Hailey. I know you value your privacy."

Hailey smiled at him reassuringly. "Yes, Sir. Thank you, Sir. I promise I'm okay. I'm only sorry the evening was spoiled for you."

The forced smile eased into something more authentic, his green eyes crinkling at the corners. "Well, other than the ending, it was a great night, and you were the star attraction, slave Hailey."

Embarrassed but pleased, Hailey set her snifter carefully on the coaster. The end table between their chairs was especially beautiful, made from a dark wood with stunning designs in lighter woods inlaid around the edges. To change the subject, Hailey remarked with sincerity, "This table is really beautiful. Is it an antique?"

Ronan shook his head. "No. I made it, actually. I made all the pieces in this room, as a matter of fact." He waved his hand to take in a large desk, several chairs and a sofa, all of it made from the same dark, lustrous wood, with intricate designs carved into the legs and arms.

"You *made* this?" Hailey was both awed and stunned by this revelation of yet another layer to this enigmatic man.

"Ronan used to be a humble carpenter, before he was 'discovered'." George drew quotations in the air around the word.

"That's how I earned my living for years," Ronan agreed. "It's what I really love doing. I miss working with my hands. I miss the peace that comes with creating beautiful, functional things."

He looked so sad as he said this that Hailey nearly asked him why he didn't return to it. She held her tongue, however, aware that, even though this evening *felt* like three friends sharing a glass of brandy after a delicious meal, she was still his hired slave girl — nothing more.

George drank the last of his drink and set his glass down. Hauling himself to his feet, he said, "Well, I'm going to head on out. I want to be first in line in the morning for the tabloids, so I can add some pictures to my scrapbook." He grinned. "Assuming I'm in any of the shots, which is doubtful."

Ronan glowered and George playfully swatted at the younger man's head. "Relax, buddy. It's no big deal. Just part of the game—you know that." He turned to Hailey and smiled. "Have a good night, sweet girl. Keep this young Master in line."

Ronan walked George to the door. Hailey waited in the hallway. It was after midnight, and normally by now she would be tucked into her little bed beside the dungeon. She touched the sleeve of her pretty dress, wondering if she should take off her clothing now that they were alone again. The night had been such an aberration, she wasn't sure what was expected of her.

Not sure what to do, she dropped to her knees and waited, head bowed. She heard Ronan's footsteps and felt his presence as he stopped to stand in front of her. He tapped her shoulder and she rose to her feet. "Take off those things," he commanded in a low, sensual voice. "All of it.

Hailey slipped off her shoes and reached back to unzip her dress. She stepped carefully out of it and placed it on the hallway side table, another beautiful piece of craftsmanship she recognized must be Ronan's.

Lifting her leg, she balanced her foot on the top of the low table, consciously posing in a way that her Master would find pleasing as she slowly rolled the silky stocking down her leg. As she shifted her position to remove the other stocking, she stole a glance at Master Ronan, and was at once gratified and thrilled to see him watching her with hungry, burning eyes.

Once completely naked, she stood at attention, arms crossed behind her back, awaiting her Master's next bidding. She expected him to tell her to go up to bed. And, in truth, she was exhausted, not used to eating so much food or drinking so much alcohol, coupled with the unwelcome excitement that had followed the meal.

Master Ronan surprised her by saying, "I want you in my bed tonight, slave Hailey. Does that suit you?"

She stood stunned for several beats. Night after night as she curled up alone in her dungeon loft, she had dreamed of falling asleep in this man's arms, not as his slave, but as his lover. Was tonight the start of something new?

Stop it, she admonished herself. *Don't anticipate, don't manipulate. Obey with grace. Answer the question.*

"Yes, Sir," she replied, hoping her voice sounded calmer than she felt. "That would suit me, Sir."

"Good."

He led her up the stairs and into his bedroom. "There should be an extra toothbrush in the bottom right drawer under the sinks," he said, waving toward the bathroom. "I'm just going to get out of my things."

Hailey went into the bathroom, ordering herself not to speculate on how many other women had opened the drawer to choose from the several wrapped toothbrushes. Ronan came in while she was washing her face and took up a position at the second sink. Hailey stole a look at him as he brushed his teeth, allowing herself a brief fantasy that they were an old married couple, shocked at how *right* it felt.

She preceded Ronan back to the bedroom. He had turned off the light, but the room was bathed in the silvery glow of the full moon coming through the large picture windows that looked out on the ocean behind the house.

Again not sure what to do, she knelt beside the bed in an at-ease position and waited, consciously clearing her mind of clutter as she invited peace to take its place. She closed her eyes and slipped into a simple meditation, taking herself back to her Vermont home. Hummingbirds flitted to and fro around the feeder she'd set up on her back porch, and the wind chimes tinkled in harmony with the rush of the creek at the edge of her property.

How she missed her little cottage, and the peace of her quiet life. Not that she would have given up the months of training at The Compound, or this incredible opportunity with Master Ronan. Deep-seated and long-held needs to submit had finally been fully explored and met with this adventure, and she didn't regret a minute of it.

If only she could have it all...

Ronan tapped her shoulder. She rose, head still bowed. He took her into his arms. She melted against his strong naked body. Ronan pressed her down onto the mattress and lay beside her, again taking her into his arms. Lifting himself on an elbow, he looked down at her. He stroked the hair from her face. "I'm sorry about tonight," he said again.

"Really, I'm okay. I promise."

He nodded and smiled ruefully. "I guess I'm the one with the problem, huh? I hadn't realized it quite so starkly before, but I hate my life." He barked a laugh and ran a hand over his eyes. "I know, that sounds so fucking entitled, right? Don't think I don't know it. I've got it all—the fame, the career, the stuff that goes with it." He shook his head. "I guess it's just not what I thought it would be. When I first got into this, I thought it would be fun—a new challenge, something completely different. But somehow I got pigeonholed into these action films, and while the pay is great, it's not really acting. It's saying three lines and then working with the stunt men to make the car crash scenes and leaping from burning building shots look realistic. I'm selling a brand—those are the actual words my agent uses, and he sees nothing wrong with that. I miss just being a regular guy who can go out with his girl without having to hide out to do it. I miss making furniture—creating something beautiful, something real."

Go out with his girl... Was she his girl? She forced herself to focus on the man, instead of her own silly fantasies. He looked so woebegone, and her heart broke a little for him.

"Permission to speak, Sir?"

He smiled sadly. "Of course, yes. Please."

"If you hate what you're doing so much, why don't you just quit?"

He snorted. "Don't think it hasn't occurred to me. It's not as easy as you think to just walk away. I'm like an *industry*, for god's sake. I'm tied in every which way. And I've *made* it. I've hit the big time, but it ain't gonna last—that's what my people, my *handlers*, are always reminding me. How can I just walk out on that?"

Hailey said nothing to this. She recognized she didn't understand the intricacies of whatever he was dealing with. This was something he would have to work through on his own. What the hell did a small town yoga instructor know about Hollywood? At the same time, she was deeply gratified that he'd felt close enough and safe enough to confide in her.

What would happen tomorrow, though, when they resumed their roles as Master and slave?

She would face that in the morning. Right now, she dared to reach for him, her heart thumping as he allowed her to pull him down into her arms. They lay quietly, and though she could feel his erection against her thigh, he made no move to claim her with his body, and gave no sign he expected anything from her.

She snuggled against him, breathing in his inviting masculine scent. Ronan lay still beside her, his eyes closed. Though she would have been ready and willing to service her Master in any way he wished, she could no longer deny the increasingly persistent tug of sleep. She closed her eyes, and dizziness assailed her, thanks to the wine and brandy still working their way through her system.

With a final sigh, she gave in, letting sleep claim her as she lay in Ronan's comforting arms.

Chapter 9

A persistent buzzing sound wormed its way into a particularly nice dream, but it was Ronan's shout that jerked Hailey fully awake. "What? What the *fuck* are you talking about! What do you mean it's all over the goddamned internet! How is that even possible?"

The room was flooded with sunlight. Ronan, in the bed beside her, held his cell phone to his ear in a white-knuckled grip. He looked hard as stone, the anger in the air around him shimmering like sudden heat. Alarmed, Hailey tensed beside him.

There was a stream of feminine chatter from the phone, during which Ronan's countenance darkened even further. "No, I will *not* tell you who she is. Are you out of your goddamned mind? I don't *want* it out there, are you insane? This is my private life, damn you. Jesus, Pat, you're my publicist. Fucking *fix* this. Get it taken down. I don't care what it takes—just *do* it."

He tapped the screen to end the call and threw the phone down onto the bed. He turned to Hailey, his face crumpling with what could only be described as mortification. "Oh, Hailey. I am so, so, so sorry."

"What's going on, Sir?" she queried, trying to keep the distress his behavior was causing at bay. Surely he was overreacting? "Is it the photos from last night? I told you, I'm okay with it. Nobody knows who I am anyway. Being linked to the famous Ronan Wolfe isn't the worst thing that could happen to a girl." She bit her lip, afraid by the sudden flash in his eyes that she'd gone too far.

"It's way worse than that. Way worse," he said ominously. His words made her stomach swoop unpleasantly, and her left temple had started to pound. He retrieved the cell phone and clicked on the screen. He held it so she could see.

"It's everywhere—apparently it hit about three in the morning, and it has gone viral. I could sue that fucking restaurant into oblivion, but what good would that do? The video is still out there. Damn it, I never should have taken you out of the house."

The video on the screen was in black-and-white. It took Hailey a moment to understand what she was seeing. "It's some kind of security camera feed," Ronan continued. "That little shit waiter must have decided to trade his job for this fucking piece of tape. The only saving grace is there's no audio, but still..."

Hailey watched with dawning horror at the image of herself walking toward the table in the private dining room they'd been in the night before. It showed her dropping to her knees and slipping under the tablecloth. Ronan's face in the video made it clear something was happening under there to him, something he liked very much.

Then the camera jumped, crudely edited to move to a shot of her beside Ronan at the table, her face flushed, lips parted, hands clenched on the table.

Hailey wanted to look away, but found she couldn't. The clip segued to Ronan sliding his hand into the top of her dress, his eyes hooded with lust as he, and the rest of the internet world, watched her shudder and tremble to orgasm.

Words flashed at the bottom of the screen: *Ronan Wolfe caught on camera with his hand in the cookie jar! WHO is the Sex-Crazed Mystery Girl who seems to be enjoying **way** more than the food at Ronan Wolfe's table? Is she a secret lover? Or just a girl toy hired for a night of dirty fun? Leave your tips regarding this sexy girl's identity at #RonanWolfeMysteryDate. Leave your comments at #HaveWhatShe'sHaving.*

The screen went blank. Hailey felt as if she had been sucker punched, all the air ripped from her lungs. Bile rose in her throat and for one horrible moment she thought she would vomit. She swallowed hard, blinking back tears.

Ronan was watching her, concern on his face, but she was unable to meet his eye. When he reached out for her, she instinctively pulled away. She didn't want to be comforted — she wanted to run away.

Rolling from the bed, she sprinted across the bedroom, barely able to hear him calling her name over the beating of her heart thumping loudly in her ears. Panting, she raced down the hallway and up the stairs to the dungeon. She could hear Ronan behind her, pounding up the stairs just a few feet away. She hurtled across the floor of the dungeon, heading for the sanctuary of her tiny bedroom. Before she could cross the threshold, he caught her from behind, pulling her back into a tight embrace, even as she struggled to break free.

She was gasping for air and tears were running in hot rivulets down her cheeks. Ronan held her close, his strong arms tight around her torso. She could feel his heart beating against her back. "Shh, calm down. It's okay. Everything is going to be okay, I promise. I was too focused on myself just now. My focus and concern should have been on you."

His tone was different than it had been down in the bedroom, deeper and calmer. The edge of furious panic she'd heard on the phone with his publicist was gone. Hailey responded to his mastery, the clench of humiliation and impotent rage loosening in her gut. She let out a tremulous breath and leaned against him, no longer fighting.

Ronan released his hold of her and spun her gently to face him. Hailey was trembling, but staring into his eyes was like gazing at the ocean, and she felt herself centering as she looked up at him. Putting his hands on her shoulders, he said, "Whatever happens out there, it's not real. It doesn't matter. What's real is what happens here and now, between us. We've had a shock. We need to re-center ourselves—to refocus." He released her shoulders and took a step back.

"I want you to use the bathroom and wash up. Then I want you to stand under the restraining beam and extend your arms. We will center ourselves with some bondage and erotic pain."

The trembling had stopped. "Yes, Sir," Hailey said gratefully. "Thank you, Sir."

After using the toilet and brushing her teeth, she returned to stand as directed in the center of the dungeon beneath the restraining beam. Ronan was waiting for her, several coils of soft white rope in his hands. She lifted her arms and allowed Master Ronan to wrap the rope around each wrist. He attached the ropes to chains that hung from the beam, and then adjusted the chains until her arms were taut overhead.

Using more rope, he wrapped it tightly around her breasts. He produced a pair of clover clamps, which he attached quickly to each nipple. The sudden shock of pain was a small, welcome explosion of release, and Hailey's responding "ah!" was met with an understanding nod by her Master.

"Feet shoulder-width apart," he ordered, and she promptly obeyed.

He drew the rope between her legs, pulling it hard against her inner labia and clit, and securing it to more rope cinched around her waist. Properly bound and clamped, Hailey let go of the last vestiges of her tension with a contented sigh.

Master Ronan left her a moment and returned holding a long, whippy cane with a black suede handle. "You will hold nothing back," he informed her. "You will give me everything you have."

"Yes, Sir," Hailey breathed.

The cane struck with a crack against her ass, the pain registering a second later and dragging a cry from her lips. He struck her again, a line of dark, pulsing fire where her ass met her thighs. The cane cut over both cheeks and crisscrossed in thwacking, whistling blows against the backs of her thighs. Hailey jerked like a marionette in her ropes, each graceless movement causing the tight, knotted rope to burn against her spread cunt. She whimpered as she struggled and twisted in her vain efforts to evade the cane's bite.

"Stop resisting," Master Ronan commanded, his voice deep as he moved behind her. "Give yourself to the pain. Give yourself to me." As he spoke, he touched the back of her neck with his hand and his lips brushed her shoulder. "You are mine," he whispered. "Show me your grace."

His words were calming, his touch like a raft in a stormy sea. She let the panic ebb away like an outgoing tide. She closed her eyes and focused on her breathing. *In…and out. Slow and calm. Flow with the pain. Embrace the pain. Become one with the pain.* She relaxed in the rope bonds, letting them support her. Her heart slowed to a steady, calm beat.

"Are you ready to continue, slave Hailey?"

"Yes, Sir."

He kissed her shoulder once more, removed his hand from her neck and stepped back. This time when the cane hit, the pain was as powerful as before, but its sting no longer cut across her serenity. She could do this for Master Ronan. She would do this for herself. She was on a cliff, arms outstretched, ready to fly. Another stroke and then another, and she tipped forward and left the ground, transforming the pain, transcending the suffering in a revelation of peace and surrender.

Later that morning as they ate breakfast, the whirring, clacking sound of helicopter blades outside the windows made conversation difficult. A glance at the kitchen security cameras trained on the perimeters of the property showed dozens of cars and TV trucks, along with reporters and paparazzi on foot milling about, cell phones, cameras and microphones at the ready, should Ronan make an appearance.

His cell phone buzzed repeatedly. He didn't take the calls, but he did respond to various texts from his agent and publicist. Finally, a disgusted look on his face, he turned off the phone. His expression was dark. "The press isn't going to let up. We're going to be hounded night and day over this. I'm so sorry to have dragged you into this."

"It wasn't your fault, Sir," Hailey tried to reassure him, though she, too, was disquieted by all the unwelcome attention. She believed him when he warned it would only get worse.

He offered a small, sad smile that broke her heart. "You didn't sign up for this." He shook his head. "We need to get out of here. Let all this hubbub die down. The only thing is, I have no idea where to go."

Hailey smiled. "I have an idea, Sir. You could come with me."

~*~

Ronan shook hands with the pilot. "Thanks again for flying us out so early and on such short notice. I really appreciate both that and your company's continued discretion."

The pilot drew a finger across his lips like a zipper. "Discretion is our byword, as always, Mr. Wolfe. Right, Carlo?" He nodded toward the flight attendant.

"Absolutely. Mum's the word. We appreciate your business, sir." Carlo released the door latch and the stairs lowered to the ground of the small Vermont county airport.

Ronan had hired this particular charter company a number of times before and was grateful they were able to accommodate his request. He and Hailey had left the Malibu house at three in the morning, slipping down the long drive with no headlights, the car packed with everything Hailey had brought, along with clothing for Ronan and, far more importantly, essential BDSM gear. They were in the air by five a.m.

California time, and with the three-hour time difference, had touched down at the small Vermont county airport at seven thirty a.m. local time.

Ronan stiffened as they deplaned, half expecting to find reporters and paparazzi waiting to accost them. Happily, no one seemed to have yet figured out he was here. Hopefully, it would stay that way for as long as possible.

A man in his sixties with a chauffeur's cap slouched against a hired car. He straightened to attention as Hailey and Ronan stepped down onto the tarmac. Carlo followed a moment later, their bags in tow. The driver hurried over. "Mr. Davenport? I'm Barney from Bennington Limo. I'll be taking you to Dorset." The man thrust out his hand.

They'd used Hailey's surname to secure the car, and Ronan didn't correct the man as they shook. "Thanks," he said, pleased to note zero recognition in the older gentleman's eyes. In fact, the man was eying Hailey, who looked lovely in her simple cotton shift. Hell, she would have looked lovely in a potato sack.

Her face was lifted to the sky, her eyes closed as if in prayer as she drew in a deep breath of the clean, crisp Vermont air. She must have felt their eyes on her, because she turned toward the men, her face breaking into a sunny smile. "It's good to be home," she said.

Barney nodded approvingly. "You from Vermont, young lady?" he said conversationally as he loaded their things into the trunk of the car.

"Born and bred," Hailey agreed.

"You, Sir?" the driver asked Ronan.

"No, I'm from Ca—" Ronan began, and then corrected himself, "from Pennsylvania. Small town near Lancaster."

"Amish country," Barney said with a nod. Scrutinizing Ronan more carefully, he added, "You don't look Amish, though." He squinted. "Wait a minute. I know you, don't I?" He tugged thoughtfully on an earlobe. His bushy eyebrows rose in sudden recognition. "Well, snatch me baldheaded! You're that fella on TV! No, wait, not TV, those movies with the car chases. Holy cow. You're a movie star." He lowered his brows and tilted his head. "But your name, your movie star name. It's not Davenport. No, it's something else." He squinted in thought. "Wild? Walton? Wood?"

"You're mistaken, sir. You have me confused with someone else, " Ronan interrupted firmly, speaking more sharply than he'd intended. The older man snapped his mouth closed, apparently having gotten the message. "We're ready to go now, thanks," Ronan continued more gently. "You have the address?"

The driver looked affronted, but then his expression eased into one of sly understanding. "Ah, okay. I get it. No problem, Mr. *Davenport*. I hear you loud and clear." With a wink, the man strode around the car and climbed into the driver's seat.

Ronan shook his head with a rueful grin. It would be what it would be. He thanked Carlo once more and waved toward the plane. He opened the back door of the car, gestured for Hailey to enter and then slid in beside her. Reaching into his pocket, he pulled out his cell phone, considered leaving it off, but decided better of it and flicked it on.

His fan club Twitter account, created at his publicist's insistence, showed 11,246 new notifications. He made a mental note to delete the account. There were twelve texts from Armand, seven from Pat and one from George. He opened that one. *Hope you guys landed okay. Everything fine here. No one even knows you're gone. Paparazzi still camped out on the edge of your property, ha ha. Let me know when you're settled.*

As the car pulled out of the small airport, Ronan shot a quick text back to his old friend to let him know they'd arrived safely. Deciding to deal with the other texts later, he turned to Hailey. She was looking out her window. He touched her leg, and she turned toward him, a small smile playing over her pretty mouth.

"You okay?"

"I'm fine, Sir. I'm good."

Ronan had managed to escape his handlers by telling them he was just slipping away for a while until the hubbub surrounding the video died down. He'd let it "slip" to his publicist and a few others that he was headed to Baja, Mexico for some much-needed rest and relaxation, aware this supposedly confidential disclosure would soon be common knowledge.

He had made a decision, one he hadn't yet shared with anyone, not Hailey, not even George. He wasn't going back to California. He wasn't going to accept the movie package deal Armand was still hounding him to sign. He wasn't going to return to the Malibu compound that had become as much a prison as a home.

For the first time in his adult life, he had no career plan. No obligations. He was grateful to Hailey for allowing him to hide out in Dorset, but had no real idea what was going to happen next. That was okay. He felt light—freed. As if he'd cast off a ten-ton weight he'd been hauling on his shoulders for years.

They drove for about thirty minutes, Hailey telling Ronan about various landmarks along the way, the happiness evident in her voice. "You haven't been back home in a while, huh?" he said, watching her rather than the scenery.

"I spent two months at The Compound," she agreed, "and then went straight to you. A neighbor stops by my place from time to time to make sure no raccoons or bears have taken up residence. So, yes, it's been a while."

"Here we are," Barney said, twisting back to regard them. "Dorset's main square. Where to now?"

As Hailey gave him specific directions to her cottage, located just outside the town, Ronan took in the area, not all that unlike his Pennsylvania boyhood home, the architecture New England white clapboard and red brick. There were lots of big, old trees and flowering foliage, everything so green after the more desert-like conditions he'd become used to in California.

The roads narrowed as they left the town, moving past marble quarries and farms. The car slowed to a crawl behind a large tractor carrying a huge bale of hay that seemed precariously piled. "Slow down a bit, please," Hailey said suddenly. "My road's just up here." Ronan could hear the quiet excitement in her voice, and her eyes were shining. Impulsively he put his arm around her. She leaned into him. He breathed in her fresh scent, his cock stirring with sudden desire for this lovely woman.

He'd spent the last seven years deflecting any attempts at something serious with a woman, telling himself and others his career came first. Now, for the first time in years, he would no longer have his work to hide behind. The past weeks as Hailey's Master had been the most fulfilling erotic and emotional experience of his life, but was it love? Did love even enter the equation when there was a negotiated contract with an end date?

They passed a couple of houses along a winding country road, each separated by an acre or more of property. At the end of the road stood a small stone house surrounded by maple trees. "This is it," Hailey announced. A red Prius was parked in the driveway, and the car pulled up behind it. Hailey jumped out of the backseat and ran to the small garden in front of the house, which was overgrown with wildflowers and clover. She knelt down and then twisted back, smiling beatifically. "The rabbit hole is still here. Looks like it's still inhabited, though I guess the last litter of babies is all grown up by now."

Barney popped the trunk and climbed out of the driver's seat. Ronan hoisted their bags out himself and reached into his pocket for his wallet. He handed the driver a fifty-dollar bill. "Thanks for driving us," he said with a cordial smile.

Barney pocketed the bill with a broad smile of his own. "Most welcome, Mr. *Davenport*," he said with another wink. "And don't worry—your secret's safe with me."

As the car drove away, Ronan hoisted the bags and walked with them toward the front door of the cottage, which was painted a bright, glossy red. A wreath of green and purple dried herbs hung at its center above a brass doorknocker.

Hailey joined him and, reaching into her small bag, produced a key, which she slid into the lock. The inside of the house was dark and cool. Hailey moved toward the windows, pulling back blue and white gingham patterned curtains to let in sunlight filtered by the many trees surrounding the property.

She turned to face him, her expression suddenly shy. "I know it's much smaller than you're used to," she said. "I've just got the one bedroom. The other has been converted into my yoga studio. I hope that's okay."

"It's more than okay," Ronan said, meaning it.

The main room contained a sofa and two matching chairs upholstered in thick stripes of blue and white arranged around the hearth, woven rag rugs scattered over wide-planked pine hardwood. There was a warmth to the place, a comfort and simplicity that pleased Ronan's sense of design.

On the fireplace mantle rested a small, exquisitely sculpted bronze statue of a female nude, her head thrown back in ecstasy. Ronan moved closer to examine it. "This is lovely," he said, running a finger over its sensuous curves. "It catches the essence of submissive grace."

"Yes, Sir. That's exactly what I always thought. I found it at an estate sale years ago, and I had to have it." She smiled.

Ronan turned back to the room. "I love your place. Did you decorate this yourself?"

"Some of it," Hailey said. "But I kept a lot of it as it's always been. This was my grandmother's home. I inherited it when she died." A small spasm of pain moved over her features.

"I'm sorry," Ronan offered.

Hailey smiled sadly. "Thank you. I still miss her every day, though it's been ten years now." She brightened. "She lived a good life, though. She died peacefully in her sleep. She was ready to go, I guess. My grandpa had died two years before, and she was lonely. He was her one true love, and she was firmly convinced he was up in heaven waiting for her." She shrugged, shaking her head. "I hope she was right."

The eat-in kitchen contained a scarred oak table and four matching chairs. The refrigerator was the only modern appliance in the place, and even that was easily forty years old. There was a wonderful antique blue porcelain gas oven and the cabinets were painted white with thick green glass windows revealing old crockery, neatly stacked and arranged.

She showed him the bedroom, which was just as he would have imagined, most of the room dominated by a big brass bed covered with an old-fashioned patchwork quilt, plenty of feather pillows piled at its head. An antique armoire took the place of a closet.

The yoga studio, located at the back of the house, was a surprise, quite different from the country décor in rest of the house. The room was furnished with a single futon couch covered in off-white canvas set in a wooden frame. A thick, dark blue yoga mat lay on the floor in the middle of the room, as if it had been waiting for Hailey's return.

The biggest surprise, though, was the front wall, which was comprised entirely of floor-to-ceiling windows. "Wow!" Ronan enthused as he stepped toward the windows. They looked out on overgrown herb and vegetable gardens edged by flowering bushes. The property sloped down toward a copse of trees. Slanting sunbeams shone through the branches, bathing the room with a coppery, almost liquescent light.

"This space is fantastic. I take it this wasn't part of the original cottage?"

"No," Hailey acknowledged. "My dad tore down this wall for my yoga studio. He's very handy around the house. He understood my need for a sense of space and light when I practice yoga. The windows are heavy duty insulated, though, since Vermont winters can be pretty intense."

Ronan nodded. His eye was drawn to the back wall, upon which were hung three large photographs, each simply framed in black, the frames spaced equidistant along the wall. He stepped closer to examine the photos. They were black-and-white, except for the rope, which had been tinted a bright, blood red when the photos were developed. The female model in the pictures was a slender woman with long hair and large, dark eyes that stared hauntingly into the camera.

She was naked, save for the red ropes, which were artfully knotted around her body in the geometric patterns and designs typical of classic Shibari rope bondage. In one of the poses, the model was standing upright in an empty room, arms behind her back, the red rope covering her torso in an intricate series of knots. In the second, the rope was wound into her long, dark hair, which was tied to a beam above her head, forcing her onto tiptoe. The third photograph was taken outside. The woman was suspended upside down from a tree, her feet and legs bound together, her body crisscrossed with the red rope, her hair streaming downward to sweep the ground.

Ronan turned to Hailey, who stood just behind him. "These are amazing," he said, awestruck. "Where did you get these?"

"I took them," Hailey said matter-of-factly. "I've always enjoyed photography. I have a friend in town who's a photojournalist. We barter—she takes yoga classes in exchange for letting me use her darkroom whenever I want. The model was an acquaintance of mine I met when I was trying to explore the scene on my own a few years back. She and her partner are heavily into Japanese rope bondage and they put on shows at a club in Burlington. They were looking for someone discreet to do a photo session, and they allowed me to keep a few of the negatives for myself." She shrugged and smiled. "It was fun, except I was jealous. I wanted to be the one getting tied up." Her smiled lifted into a grin.

"Your wish is my command, my lady," Ronan said with a mock bow and a return grin. "Seriously, though, you are quite a talented photographer. I love what you did with the rope color. Do you have other work?"

"I do," Hailey replied. "Though it's mostly just honey bees and hummingbirds. A few bunny rabbits. I don't usually do people, but I made an exception for her."

"Well, you have quite an artist's eye, Hailey. I'm very impressed."

"Thank you, Sir." Hailey beamed happily. Ronan turned to take in the rest of the room. "This is an amazing space. I see a lot of potential for this room, as these photos suggest." He moved closer to her and placed a finger lightly beneath her chin, lifting her face to his. "I know some Shibari, slave girl. You would be beautiful bound like that model. Is this room solely for yoga or..." He let the sentence hang, his finger still beneath her chin.

"It's for whatever pleases you, Sir," she whispered, her pupils dilating and her lips parting as she stared into his eyes.

He took her face into his hands and dipped his head to kiss her. Since he'd invited her into his bed, despite all the insanity of the past twenty-four hours, something had shifted between them. They were still Master and slave, yes, but there was more at play now—a deepening to the relationship he hoped wasn't just on his side.

As he kissed her, he slipped the straps of her dress down her shoulders, pushing at the fabric of her light dress until her lovely high breasts were revealed. Letting go of her mouth, he ducked to capture one of her nipples with his teeth. He bit lightly, and then a little harder, loving the swell of her engorging nipple against his tongue, and the sensual breathy sigh in her throat.

He pushed her gently to the ground, angling her so they were on the thick, soft yoga mat. He pulled at her dress, dragging it from her body. With his permission, she had worn underwear during the flight, and he yanked these aside as well.

He knelt up between her legs, pushing them open, and leaned down to inhale her spicy sweetness. She started to close her legs. "Oh, Sir, you don't have to. I mean—"

He stopped her with a finger to her lips. "I do what I want. I take what I want, slave Hailey. I want this. It is mine, is it not?"

Her cheeks were flushed, her dark blue eyes bright. Slowly she nodded, letting her thighs fall open. "Yes, Sir. Excuse me, Sir. I forgot myself for a moment."

"You did," Ronan agreed. "You will be punished later. For now, however, I want to taste you." He leaned forward and snaked his tongue along her already-slick labia and circled her clit. As he licked and suckled her cunt, her moans of ecstasy fueled his passion. He didn't stop until she cried out, "Please, Sir, oh god, please! May I come, Sir, oh! May I please, please come?"

"You may." She shuddered and moaned as he held her fast. He kissed the insides of her thighs with a hundred tiny kisses as she lay, legs akimbo, face and throat flushed with orgasm, chest heaving. When she finally stilled, he leaned back on his haunches, wiped his mouth with the back of his hand, and waited.

She opened her eyes and looked up at him. He rubbed the front of his jeans. "I'm in need of attention now, slave girl," he said, his stern tone belied by his smile.

"Oh, yes, Sir, right away, Sir!" Hailey scrambled to her knees. Ronan stood in front of her and put his hands on his hips, watching as she unzipped his fly and pulled his jeans and underwear down to his knees. She took his cock hungrily into her mouth, her hands stroking and cupping his balls as she licked and sucked him to perfection. It might have been minutes, but it felt more like seconds before he was ready to spurt. He gripped the sides of her head and rammed his shaft deeply into her throat, the power of his position as thrilling as the feel of her silky lips and tongue on his cock. He held her that way until he'd spilled every drop.

Finally letting her go, he stared down at her, a strange almost painful combination of lust and love twisting through him like a blade.

"Thank you, Sir," she said softly.

"Thank you, slave girl," he replied. He pulled up his jeans and extended a hand, helping Hailey to her feet. He drew her into his arms and kissed her. "You please me," he said softly into her ear. He realized he hadn't given the whole mystery girl viral video crap they'd left back in California a single thought since they'd stepped foot inside Hailey's peaceful little cottage. "And this place pleases me," he added. "Thank you for inviting me here. I do appreciate it."

He let her go. She smiled at him. "You're very welcome. To tell you the truth, I hadn't realized how much I missed being here until now. It's good to be home. Oh!" she said suddenly. "I haven't given you the full tour yet. Would you like to see out back? There's a workshop out there you might want to check out. Some of the stuff in there is really old. It belonged to my grandpa."

"Sure," Ronan agreed. "I'd love to see it."

Hailey reached for her dress, and then looked up at Ronan for permission. He nodded. "You can put that back on—for now."

He followed her into the small kitchen and out onto a wrap-around back porch. Off to the side of the property was another stone structure about the size of a large shed. They walked to it, and Hailey pushed open the unlocked door. Though the room had two small, high windows, it still needed the overhead light that she flicked on with a switch just inside the door.

Ronan took in the space, transported by the sight of it to another time and place, before the world had known he existed, when he was just a simple carpenter trying to make a living with his hands and his back. Something eased inside him as he looked around the room—a tightly coiled wire of tension at his core slowly unspooling.

"Wow, some of this stuff is from the turn of the last century," he said, not trying to hide the awe he felt. It was clear the person who had kept this workshop had loved and cherished his equipment.

Though coated with dust, every tool was in its place. A foot-powered grindstone stood like a Paleolithic bicycle in the middle of the floor, complete with a stone wheel and an iron seat. Nearby stood an anvil. There was a bench with several vises waiting in a row, and a paint locker filled with cans of paint and stain neatly lined and labeled. On the pegboard wall were carpenter's tools, each hung within its drawn outline. There were hammers, sledges, wooden and rubber mauls, hatchets, axes, screwdrivers, chisels, hacksaws, keyhole saws, pulp saws, rip and crosscut saws. In the corner stood rakes, hoes, shovels and even an old scythe. Along the top of the workbench there was a shelf of capped and labeled mason jars filled with nails, wood screws, bolts, rivets, brads and tacks.

"This is amazing," Ronan said, turning to Hailey, his face splitting into a smile so wide it hurt his cheeks.

Hailey laughed. "You look so happy, Sir. I honestly don't think I've ever seen you this happy before. I'm thinking what yoga is for me, carpentry is for you."

"I'm thinking you're right," Ronan agreed, feeling warm to his bones. He reached for her and pulled her into his arms. Hailey came willingly, lifting her face sweetly for a kiss.

But after a moment, she pulled away. "Come on," she said, an unmistakable touch of coquetry in her grin that Ronan found quite intoxicating. "I want to show you my favorite spot by the creek." Without waiting for his answer, she stepped outside and looked over her shoulder at him, her smile flung backward like a handful of flowers.

Chapter 10

Ronan stepped outside and reached for Hailey's hand. It slipped neatly into his grip, her fingers curling around his as if they'd been cast together in the same mold. They moved down a well-worn path. As they approached the creek, the sound of the water tumbling over the stones calmed Hailey.

"I can see why you love it here," Ronan said. "I haven't felt this relaxed in ages."

It was an unusually warm day even for July, the temperatures edging into the high eighties, the air more humid than what Ronan was no doubt used to from his years in California. She led him a few yards down to a flat clearing by the water, stopping beneath a cluster of trees that canopied the space in a latticework of leaves and branches. Ronan started to sit.

"Wait," Hailey said. "Let me get the blanket."

"The blanket?" Ronan turned toward her with a questioning glance.

"Yeah. My grandfather used to fish down here. My dad and brother too. I don't fish, but I kept the gear here, I guess for old time's sake. I have my own supplies here, too." Hailey moved to the large wooden storage bin that her grandfather had built back when he and her grandmother had been newlyweds. The key was in the padlock, which served to keep out curious raccoons and the occasional bear who might meander down this way from the woods.

She opened the lock and lifted the heavy lid, which still rose smoothly on its old but solid hinges. Reaching in, she pulled out a large plastic container and set it on the ground beside the bin. She removed the lid and took out the faded old quilt, along with two bottles of water and a vacuum-sealed packet of dried fruit and nuts.

Ronan helped her spread the blanket over the wild grass, and they sat side-by-side, facing the water. Hailey handed Ronan a bottle of water. She tore open the snack bag and set it between them.

"I didn't realize how hungry I was," Ronan said as he munched between sips of water. "That meal on the plane is just a distant memory. I'll need to build my strength back up so I can punish you properly for your infraction back in the yoga room." He flashed a grin in her direction as he reached casually for another handful of fruit.

"Oh." Hailey brought a hand to her mouth, feeling heat move over her cheeks at his reminder, while her nipples perked perversely against her dress.

Ronan laughed. "You thought I forgot, huh?" He shook his head, the smile falling away. He glanced around the glade. "Is this private? No neighbors?"

"No neighbors, Sir. It's very secluded. No one comes back here."

Ronan nodded. "Good. We need to reestablish some guidelines. Stand up, slave Hailey. Strip and present yourself for inspection." His blade of a stare pinned her to the spot. "Now," he added softly, though there was iron beneath the word.

Hailey's heart slipped into a higher gear, the blood revving in her veins. She rose to a standing position and slipped her sandals from her feet. She pushed at the straps of her dress and let it slide silkily down her body. Lifting her arms, she laced her fingers behind her neck and elongated her spine to an at-attention position, back arched, breasts thrust forward, legs shoulder-width apart.

Ronan pushed himself to his feet and moved closer. "Offer your cunt," he commanded.

Hailey rolled her hips forward, tilting her sex upward. Ronan reached for her mons, cupping and gripping her. His fingers stroked roughly along her labia, one digit pressing inside. "Why do you need to be punished, slave girl?"

Hailey drew in a quick breath, the usual dichotomy at war inside her. She hated to be punished. Or more accurately, she hated to engage in the kind of behavior that led to punishment—the resistance, the lack of grace, the failure to perform to her Master's dictate—and the humiliation that followed with the knowledge she had let him down. Yet at the same time she craved the attention and focus that were part and parcel of a punishment. Her natural instinct was to not only accept, but to embrace, the justly meted discipline.

"I resisted you, Sir."

"Be more specific."

"I closed my legs to you, Sir. I protested that you didn't have to do something, instead of simply obeying. I forgot my place as your slave and your possession, Sir."

"That I didn't have to do something," Ronan echoed. "Be more specific. Tell me precisely what it was you didn't want me to do."

How like Master Ronan to hone in on what was difficult for her. She realized she both loved and hated him for this. She willed away the blush threatening to wash over her cheeks. "I didn't want you to lick my pussy, Sir."

He withdrew his hand from between her legs. Stepping back, he reached for her breasts, first cupping them in his palms, then gripping her nipples between thumbs and forefingers. He twisted, gradually increasing the pressure until she winced. "Why didn't you want that, slave? Think before you answer and speak with honesty. I want to understand."

Hailey's nipples were throbbing, her cunt spasming with need, in spite of the recent orgasm. She couldn't stop the quiet but audible moan that escaped her lips as she stared up into her Master's eyes, which glittered with an inner fire of their own. Startled by the intensity of his gaze, she looked away.

Finally he released the pressure on her nipples, and Hailey's mind cleared enough to formulate a response. She looked again into his handsome face. "I love to serve, Sir, but I sometimes have a hard time receiving."

"I understand. Go on." Though the lust still shone in his eyes, so, too, did the compassion, and Hailey fell a little more in love at that moment.

Pushing the feeling aside, she forced herself to focus on what she needed to say. She understood being an erotic slave meant more than just giving one's body. The heart and mind had to follow as well. "I guess it's easier to give. You don't put yourself out there in the same way. It's less, um" — she paused as she struggled for the word — "vulnerable." Again he nodded his understanding. Still in her at-attention pose, Hailey continued, "I've never felt entirely comfortable allowing a man, especially a Dom, to lick my pussy and bring me to orgasm in that way. It feels so — so greedy, I guess. So solely about my own pleasure to the exclusion of my Master's."

"You don't believe this act provides pleasure for a man? For a Master?"

"I—I guess not really, Sir." Hailey blew out a breath, and then admitted something she hadn't even thought about for years, at least not consciously. "My first boyfriend, Chris, he told me..." She swallowed hard, the words dying in her throat. Blinking back sudden tears of shame she hadn't realized she still carried, she looked down at her feet.

"Hailey." Ronan's tone was gentle. Using a finger, her lifted her chin and looked into her eyes. "Stand at ease, arms at your sides. I can see something is troubling you. Something important. I want to hear this—to understand it. Hold nothing back. If it helps you, consider this part of your punishment."

Hailey nodded. "Yes, Sir. Thank you, Sir." She dropped her arms and let her mantra envelop her: *Serenity. Peace. Submission. Grace.* Calmed, she continued, "I was seventeen, a senior in high school. Something of a late bloomer, I guess. Chris was the most gorgeous guy in school. He was on the football team, typical jock, not my type at all, but he asked me out, and I said yes. We went out a few times, and I guess I was flattered more than anything else. It was weird but cool to be suddenly popular, even if the attention was just reflected.

"Anyway, we made out in the back of his truck a few times after going to the movies or whatever, and he was kind of dominant, though he wasn't actively into the scene or anything. I mean, neither was I, of course, but I had all the fantasies, all the hardwiring of a submissive and sexual masochist, even back then.

"It must have been the third or fourth time we were making out, and he said he wanted me to suck him off. To that point all we'd done was some heavy petting. I wasn't ready, even though most the girls in my class had progressed way beyond that. I said no, which pissed him off. He said, okay, if I wouldn't do that, I had to at least let him see me naked. Fully naked, as a way to make up for being frigid—his term."

"Hah!" Ronan interjected. "What an ass."

Hailey nodded her agreement. "Of course, in retrospect I should have told him to go fuck himself. But I was insecure and still star-struck by his popularity, and his choosing *me* for whatever reason, so I went along with it. We went to this secluded place after school one day, and I stripped for him and propped myself against the car door.

"He crouched in front of me and really examined my pussy, his face up close. I got self-conscious and I tried to close my legs, but he stopped me by putting his hands on my thighs and telling me to hold still." She blew out a breath. "So, um, he said he wanted to *eat* me." She wrinkled her nose. "I've always hated that expression."

"Me too." Ronan agreed with a scowl. "Go on."

"I admit it, I was pretty curious what it would be like. I'd only ever come with my own hand at that point. I was nervous, but I said okay. And then he..." She trailed off, closing her eyes a moment as the painful memory washed over her.

"Go on," Ronan encouraged softly.

Hailey opened her eyes. "He said I..." Her mouth worked but no words came out. She willed the words to come. "He brought his face right up between my legs and then he kind of reared back with a sneer." She pressed her lips together, surprised the memory still carried such a sting. "Gosh, this is harder than I thought it would be to say out loud, even after all these years."

Ronan lifted his hand and stroked Hailey's cheek. "It's ancient history, but it's still got a hold on you. Go on. Get it out, and then we can let it go together."

Hailey leaned gratefully into his touch. She steeled herself for her next words. "He said I stank— that I smelled like rotten fish," she finally managed, fixing her eyes on the clear water rushing nearby. "He said maybe if I hit the showers before stripping for him like a whore, he might reconsider." Hailey hugged herself a moment, before recalling she was still supposed to be in position.

As she dropped her arms, Ronan reached for her, gathering her into a comforting embrace. "I apologize, Hailey. I apologize for the whole male population. And just for the record, beautiful girl, your scent is intoxicating, and your cunt is absolutely beautiful."

Letting her go, he stepped back, shaking his head with disgust. "That guy was nothing but a stupid, insecure punk. I bet if the little chickenshit had pulled down his pants, you'd have found pimples on his ass, not to mention piss stains and shit tracks on his tighty-whities. But don't think for a second he'd have had the slightest qualms about ramming his sweaty dick down your throat for all twelve seconds it took before he prematurely ejaculated."

Hailey burst into startled laughter. Ronan's mouth quirked into a smile as he watched her. He began to laugh too, a big belly laugh that made Hailey laugh harder. They both sank to the blanket, still laughing. Ronan reached for her, once more pulling her into his arms. Their laughter slowly subsided into chuckles, but then the vivid picture Ronan had created of Chris Bell, reduced now to the teenage jerk he, in fact, had been, rose in her mind's eye, and Hailey began to laugh again until tears were rolling down her cheeks. Her laughter set Ronan off again.

Finally they both quieted. Hailey felt a deep sense of peace moving over her, the kind of peace that comes not only from a good, hard laugh or cry, but from finally and truly letting go of something that had quietly but insidiously festered inside her all these years.

"Thank you," she whispered to Ronan.

He pulled her closer. "You're welcome," he whispered back. They were quiet a while longer, both staring into the mesmerizing flow of the tumbling creek. While it didn't hold a candle to Pacific Ocean in terms of size, its effect was just as peaceful and, for Hailey, far more personal and inviting.

Ronan lay back on the blanket and put his hands behind his head as a pillow. Hailey lay down beside him. She felt her eyelids begin to droop. It had been a long day, and she was exhausted. She stole a sidelong glance at Ronan. His eyes were closed, his expression relaxed, a nice contrast to the worry lines that had furrowed his forehead since the video from the restaurant had hit in the internet.

She snuggled against him, resting her head on his chest. She was nearly asleep when she heard him say, "Don't think I forgot your punishment, slave girl. After our nap, you'll select a nice whippy branch from one of these trees to use as a switch, and I'll remind you who's in charge here."

Hailey's eyes flew open, sleep banished for the moment as her skin tingled in anticipation of his promise.

~*~

It took two days before the media hounds and paparazzi found a new angle on the story. In a way, Ronan was surprised it had taken them so long to uncover something about his secret life, despite his efforts over the years at total discretion. Oddly, he wasn't nearly as upset as he supposed he should be. In a way, he was kind of relieved.

Hailey was resting beside him in the bed. She lay on her stomach, her face cradled in her arms. His heart contracted with both pleasure and pride as he regarded her. He ran his fingers lightly over the welts on her ass and thighs he'd placed there with a single tail earlier that morning. Hailey sighed sleepily, her mouth curling into a soft smile as he touched her, though her eyes remained closed.

The peace of the past few days was like none Ronan had experienced in his life, and while he hated to disturb it with this phone call, he could no longer put off the inevitable. In fact, he was ready, even eager, to let his handlers know he'd come to a decision.

Reaching for his cell phone, he pushed the speed dial for his agent. Armand picked up on the first ring. "Ronan, finally! Jesus H. Fucking *Christ*, where the hell are you? And don't tell me Baja. I've checked every damn hotel and resort in the place. Damn it, you can't just fucking disappear like that! Tell me you are back in LA. Tell me you've come to your senses, for crying out loud. I can't believe you bailed on me like this. Do you have any fucking *idea* what a cluster fuck you've left for me and Pat to fix?"

"Armand, there's something you need —" Ronan began, but Armand overrode him.

"I could actually forgive you for that little, uh, indiscretion with the mystery girl. The buzz over that has been better than any advertising campaign. Who is she anyway? I know, I know, you're a man of honor, blah, blah, blah. Actually, that can work to our advantage. Or it *could* have, before this latest mess. But now you've gone too far, Wolfe. Way the fuck too far! Have you *seen* the latest pictures of you that have surfaced on the internet?"

"Yes. I've seen them. That's why I'm calling." It had been something of a shock to see those photos, which must have been surreptitiously taken by some scumbag at The Exchange Club during one of Ronan's training sessions there. Cameras and cell phones were strictly forbidden in the club for just this reason, and until now at least, the place was known for the utmost discretion. Clearly someone had circumvented the system, and then sold the pictures for god only knew how much money to the ever-hungry media. The pictures were several months old—maybe the person who took them didn't realize what they had at first, or maybe whatever gossip rag bought them had been biding their time for the most impact. While there was nothing all that compromising in the photos, at least not in Ronan's estimation, the media was having a field day with them.

"Are they really you?" Armand demanded. "*Please*, tell me they're photo-shopped. We might be able to salvage something from this—claim someone stuck your head on some random pervert's body. Please tell me it's not really you. Tell me you're not into this sick shit. I'm begging you."

Despite his promise to himself to remain calm, Ronan was becoming annoyed. "Armand, stop it. It's not like I'm killing babies or something. This is a consensual lifestyle, and those pictures were taken without my knowledge or per—"

"Holy shit!" Armand interrupted, his voice rising in an incredulous squeal. "Am I really fucking hearing this? Having whores suck you off at restaurants isn't bad enough? Now you're into sadomasochistic sicko weird shit? America's squeaky-clean action hero is into whips and chains? Are you fucking *kidding* me?"

"Armand, listen to me—"

"No, you listen to me. I *made* you, Wolfe. I got you those initial auditions when no one else would touch you. I've worked with a whole team of professionals to sell the Ronan Wolfe brand, and you are *not* going to fuck it up, you hear me? The producers on the *True American Hero* series are threatening to pull out. Damn it, I told you to sign that fucking contract two *months* ago and now your hemming and hawing might end up costing us millions. Billions!"

Armand actually paused to take a breath, or maybe he was having a heart attack—Ronan wasn't sure. Each round of spluttering invective the man spewed only solidified Ronan's decision. He waited a beat to see if Armand was done ranting.

Apparently he wasn't, though at least his tone was slightly less hysterical. "Here's what's going to happen, Ronan. Pat wrote a brilliant press release you will personally issue. We can call a press conference, just like the president does. We'll just need one camera guy. We'll keep it simple. You will, of course, deny everything and apologize profusely to your shocked and disillusioned public for the smear campaign that's been leveled against you. "If there's a god, maybe the producers won't pull out, and we can salvage this thing somehow. Who knows" — he barked a laugh— "maybe in the long run it will even help your career. Good boy has a bad side, that sort of thing. If you can't clean it up, then make damn sure you are so, so fucking sorry for having let down your fans. That's key here."

Ronan shook his head and found he was smiling, if somewhat wryly. How in the world had he let this man run his life for so many years?

He understood Armand's concern at the impact these latest photos might have on his acting career, but why should he hide who and what he truly was? Why should he be made to feel shame and remorse because of his sexual orientation and consensual lifestyle?

Maybe a decade ago, hell, even a year ago, he might have been freaking out over the recent events in the media, but now he found he honestly didn't care. Though he didn't want the BDSM club where he'd trained compromised in any way, he was done keeping his real life a secret. Let his detractors and his so-called fans make what they would of the stolen images. He frankly didn't give a damn.

He glanced over at Hailey. She was awake now, watching him with those lovely dark blue eyes, the very picture of submissive grace and serenity.

"Well?" Armand demanded. "What do you have to say for yourself?"

"Just one thing." He paused for dramatic emphasis. "I quit."

Chapter 11

Ronan lay in the bed listening to the chirp of birds outside the open window. Hailey was already up, and he could hear the sound of eggs being whisked in a glass bowl. The warm, yeasty aroma of baking biscuits wafted into the bedroom, along with the inviting smell of frying bacon.

Since he'd escaped to Vermont, Ronan found his appetite was as hearty as a lumberjack's. He preferred Hailey's down-home cooking to the artfully crafted and prepared dishes his chef had worked so painstakingly to prepare for him back in California. Though Ronan no longer had a private gym, he kept fit by clearing away the brush and deadwood on the property, and chopping and stacking seasoned wood in preparation for the winter.

Hailey had returned to the yoga studio in town for several days a week. With her blessing, Ronan had cleared out some of the older, unusable equipment and tools in Hailey's grandfather's workshop, a workshop he was increasingly coming to think of as his own. He'd bought a few new tools and some supplies, and was at work on a set of dining room chairs to replace the spindly, rickety chairs that presently sat around her kitchen table.

He had become a regular at the two local lumberyards and the reclamation center that served as a dumping ground for the many antique stores in the area. Though he routinely wore a baseball cap and sunglasses in an effort to remain incognito, word had gotten out locally as to his identity, but the townspeople were respectful of his privacy, which was a welcome change from what he'd come to expect back in Hollywood. Thankfully, no one had yet connected the mystery girl in the internet video to Hailey, and as interest in it faded, hopefully they never would.

Hailey and he talked about how they would handle it if the connection was ever made among people she knew. Hailey had surprised and impressed him with her philosophical attitude. "This may be a relatively small town, but Vermont is a surprisingly liberal state and folks aren't nearly so judgmental as you might think. And if they do judge" — she had shrugged and smiled — "it's really their problem, not mine."

As Armand had predicted, there had been some noise and fallout over the leaked photos from the club, but with BDSM erotica moving steadily into the mainstream consciousness over the past few years, it had been less of an issue than his agent, or rather his ex-agent, had feared. Word of Ronan's retirement from acting had made more of a splash, but the speculation now was that it was just a publicity stunt. Time, he supposed, would give lie to that particular rumor.

Now, at thirty-four, he was in the extraordinary position of being independently wealthy, and able to do what actually made him happy, with no strings attached. And what made him happy was being with Hailey, and returning to his passion of creating things with his hands.

He'd been both startled and pleased at how easily his carpentry sense came back to him, even after all these years. Time ceased while he was working, and he sawed, shaved, sanded and whittled, as much by instinct as finite measure, to create the shape of the piece he saw in his head. The scent of small engine oil, wood shavings, and especially of the homemade concoction of beeswax and china wood oil he liked to use took him back to happier days. What amazed him was not how easily he'd said goodbye to his acting career and everything that went with it, but that it had taken him so long to do it.

After a quick shower, Ronan pulled on some running shorts and walked into the kitchen. Hailey was just scooping eggs onto two plates already piled with crisp bacon. Ronan came up behind her. Pushing aside her hair, he kissed the nape of her neck. She leaned back against him a moment, and then set the pan back on the stove.

"Perfect timing," she said, turning toward him with a smile. "Breakfast is served."

As they ate, Roman remarked in a casual tone, "When you come home from the studio this afternoon, I want you to strip and present yourself in the yoga room. Today we will explore your fantasies regarding Shibari rope bondage."

Hailey touched the new leather slave collar he'd fashioned for her, her mouth opening in a small O. He had come to recognize the gesture as one of nervous but eager anticipation. Like all subs he'd ever worked with, she responded as much to the anticipatory expectation of bondage and discipline as to the acts themselves.

"Yes, Sir," she murmured throatily, and his cock jutted against his shorts with anticipation of its own.

Once she had dressed and gone, Ronan went to his workshop. He lifted the St. Andrew's cross he'd designed precisely to her dimensions onto a hand truck and strapped it in place. He wheeled it to the house and positioned it front of the huge picture windows. As he ran his hand over the smooth wood, he imagined Hailey naked and bound against it, the sunlight illuminating her from behind. Soon he would make that image a reality.

He returned to the workshop to check the rope he'd been working on the past week, pleased to find it was dry and ready for use. He'd bought a large hank of hemp, but had decided it was too rough to use on Hailey's soft skin. So, after doing a little research, he'd purchased an industrial-sized pot from a kitchen supply company. Earlier that week, when Hailey was at her in-town studio, he'd boiled the rope in a special solution and it had dried as soft as silk, but much stronger. As a finishing touch, he'd dyed the rope a rich, dark red, the same color she'd used when developing the film for her Shibari photos.

He coiled the rope and hoisted it over his shoulder. Returning to the yoga studio, he cut the rope into various lengths, using the bondage sheers he'd brought with him from California. As he worked, he imagined Hailey artfully bound in the knotted rope, her face softening in that way it did when desire and submission overtook her. He started to reach into his pocket for his cell phone to check the time, and then smiled when he realized he'd forgotten even to turn it on that morning, much less put it in his pocket. Instead, he looked out the windows and gauged from the angle of the sun that Hailey would be home in about an hour.

He couldn't wait.

~*~

Hailey's skin was glowing from head to toe, as if it had been slathered in a warm, honey-like substance. The session on the new, beautiful St. Andrew's cross had been slow and sensual, the intensity gradually increasing from the first swishing strokes of soft leather through the stinging graze of the dozens of sturdy tresses to the hard, thudding beat of a full body flogging. She had turned inward at that point, drifting in a haze of sensation, occasionally pulled back to the world by an especially powerful stroke. She'd been lost in the white drift of utter peace when she was recalled to the world by her Master's low, sensual voice.

"Now that your skin is properly sensitized to receive the rope, I want to bind you. Are you ready, slave Hailey?"

Her eyes moved toward the coils of red rope waiting on the yoga mat. "Yes, Sir. I'm ready." Though her voice sounded calm, a surge of adrenaline kicked its way through her bloodstream. Master Ronan had bound her in the past, but this was the first time they would engage in an extended Shibari session, and Hailey had been thinking of little else since his statement that morning that today was the day.

As an added element of excitement, the session would take place outside in the glade. Ronan had remembered her wistful remark when they talked about her photo shoot of the Shibari session that she would have rather been the subject than just the recorder of the event. Today her wish was going to become a reality.

Master Ronan released her cuffs and helped Hailey from the cross. While she watched, he unzipped his gear duffel bag and placed the coils of red rope inside. He stood, hoisting the bag over his shoulder.

Hailey followed him through the house to the backdoor, and outside into the late afternoon sun. They moved together toward the clearing by the creek. Hailey retrieved the quilt from the bin while Master Ronan removed the rope, the bondage sheers and his cell phone from the gear bag. Hailey wondered at the phone, but didn't voice her question. She was content to wait quietly as Master Ronan spread the quilt and arranged the items. She was enjoying the play of the coppery sunlight on the water as she basked in the lingering afterglow of the flogging. A school of tiny silvery fish flashed through the rushing water. Two hummingbirds flitted in tandem through the trees.

"Slave Hailey, present yourself." The command was soft and light as a summer breeze, and pulled her gaze back to her Master like a pair of strong hands. "We will start with you standing, legs shoulder-width apart, wrists to opposite elbow behind your back in a classic box position. Once I have you secured in a way that pleases me, I will suspend you from that branch."

Master Ronan pointed to a thick sturdy branch of Hailey's favorite maple. The branch arced over the space as if it had been waiting all these decades for just this moment. A large steel Shibari ring hung from the branch by a noose of strong rope, rigged in such a way it could be raised and lowered via a simple suspension pulley system she guessed her master carpenter had designed in his workshop.

Hailey assumed her position beneath the branch. Crouching in front of her, Master Ronan secured thick leather cuffs around each of her ankles. She was surprised by how soft the rope was. As it was knotted and tightened against her flesh, she felt herself sliding into that peaceful, quiet place where bondage always took her.

Master Ronan worked quickly and silently, moving around her body as he created intricate patterns against her skin. The rope wrapped and tightened around her breasts, harnessing them in a restricting crisscross of soft red hemp. His fingers left trails of electric desire over her skin as he wound and knotted the rope between her legs. Its pull created a friction of sensation that made her clit pulse each time he tied another knot along her body.

As the rope wound up, down and around every part of her body, her heartbeat slowed to a hushed, deliberate rhythm. She became a part of the intricate pattern of rope art, a living sculpture of erotic submission, completely immobilized in her bonds.

Finally satisfied, Master Ronan stepped back and regarded her with an appraising gaze. Hailey's cunt spasmed with lust as she gazed back at her Master. He was wearing only a pair of white shorts, his bronzed, muscular body gleaming with a faint sheen of sweat, his dark hair falling into his clear green eyes.

Bending down, he reached for his cell, and held it in her direction. "I want to take pictures so you can see how breathtaking you are at this moment."

Hailey experienced a sudden twist of anxiety, the unwelcome memory of the internet video worming its way into her consciousness. As if reading her mind,

Ronan smiled gently, adding, "For our eyes only, sweet girl. I promise."

"Of course, Sir," Hailey consented with a nod, sorry she'd let her emotions show on her face. She focused on letting the calm reassert itself as Ronan moved around her body in a slow circle, the phone's camera clicking every few seconds.

He slipped the phone into his shorts pocket and moved closer to her. Taking her face in his hands, he kissed her mouth, a brush of lips against lips that left her longing for more.

"I'm going to suspend you now. First I'll lie you down flat so I can attach the rigging apparatus to your ankle cuffs." He placed his arms at her back and behind her legs and lifted her into the air, settling her down on her stomach on the quilt. He adjusted a few of the knots, his breath skimming along her skin like kisses as he worked. Moving to her legs, he wound more rope, binding them into a single unit.

Finally satisfied, he stood and reached for the rigging. He lifted Hailey slowly, turning the pulley until she was suspended upside down from the branch, her hair trailing on the ground as she swayed gently in her bonds. He stepped back and reached once more for his phone. Hailey let her eyes close as he snapped more pictures, moving around her to capture her image from all angles.

The blood rushed to her head as she swayed gently in her tight cocoon, but she didn't feel the slightest bit panicked. Instead, a deep sense of peace flooded through her, even more profound than what she experienced after an erotic whipping. When she felt herself being slowly lowered once more to the quilt, she wanted to protest that it was too soon—she would have happily remained suspended and bound for hours. She made no protest, however, aware that her Master could better gauge her tolerance level at this point than she could.

She lay quietly on the quilt, eyes still closed, as he unknotted and removed the rope from her body, making her feel like a precious package being slowly and sensually unwrapped. She shivered slightly as the cooling air brushed her naked body. Master Ronan rolled her gently to her back. She opened her eyes when he placed his hands on her thighs and gently pushed them apart. She stiffened when he lowered his face to her pussy, but then she recalled herself.

She belonged to this man. She would withhold nothing from him. She spread her legs and gave herself to his kiss.

It didn't take long before a powerful orgasm cascaded its way through her body with such sudden force she barely had time to gasp for permission to come. The permission was granted, and she let herself be carried away by her lover's perfect touch.

She lay panting for several long moments until Master Ronan said, "Turn over. Lift yourself on your hands and knees and offer your ass to me. I want to take what's mine."

Again a small blade of anxiety twisted its way through her gut. They'd been working off and on with her full acceptance of ass play. Though she wanted to give of herself fully, so far she'd never quite managed it. Even if she'd given her body, a small part of her psyche still resisted. Nevertheless, she obediently turned over and knelt as ordered, legs spread wide, forehead resting against the quilt, ass high.

She felt the cold dollop of lubricant between her cheeks, and a moment later the insistent nudge of Ronan's cock. She was suddenly overcome with a submissive love so powerful she thought it might consume her. Reaching back, she spread her ass cheeks in offering. She needed to give of herself in this way — to show the man she loved that she would hold nothing back from him.

"Please," she begged, "fuck me in the ass, Sir. Please."

"Hands behind your back, wrists crossed," Ronan commanded, and Hailey instantly obeyed. He gripped her hips, the growl low and feral in his throat as he pushed himself slowly but inexorably into her tight opening. Hailey pushed back against him, for the first time not only willing, but eager for his gift as he filled her.

She gave of herself completely, holding nothing back as he thrust and moved inside her. "I want you to come with me," he murmured into her ear. When he reached around her body and stroked her sopping cunt, she exploded in an orgasm so powerful she thought it might lift them both from the ground. Ronan cried out in his passion. They fell forward, Ronan pinning Hailey beneath his masculine weight as they collapsed together on the quilt. They lay that way for some time, until he finally rolled away.

Reaching for Hailey, he gathered her into his arms. "Hailey," he said softly, his lips brushing her ear. "I love you. I've been waiting for you all my life, though I didn't know it. I have a question for you. You don't have to answer right now, if you don't want."

Hailey, who had been luxuriating in her Master's strong embrace, opened her eyes, instantly curious what the question might be, already certain she would agree to anything this man asked of her. "Yes, Sir?"

His expression was tender, his eyes burning with an inner fire. "Will you be my wife?"

Chapter 12

Ronan could feel Hailey's excitement as they waited at the door of the beautifully restored farmhouse. The whole compound looked more like a gracious horse farm than a BDSM club, with its rolling pastures, an old paddock and stables visible behind the main building. Ronan put his arm around Hailey as they turned to take in the idyllic view. "So, this is where it all happened, huh? It's hard to believe a place like this even exists." Though George had been to The Compound several times on Ronan's behalf, this was Ronan's first visit to the upstate New York slave training facility.

The timing had been perfect. Mistress Miriam had contacted Ronan the week before to see how things were going with slave Hailey, and upon discovering they were only a few hours away, invited the two of them to visit for the weekend. Hailey had eagerly agreed she would love to return.

"I made some good friends there," she had explained. "Not just with some of the other slave girls in training, but with some of the staff slaves, especially one named Alexis—she's owned by Paul, a terrific trainer. I got to work with him on endurance and grace training. He was *amazing*." She'd sounded so fervently sincere in this proclamation that Ronan had almost been jealous. "They have a first-rate chef there too. You'll love the food. And it's such a nurturing environment—filled with likeminded people who not only understand, but fully embrace the BDSM lifestyle. Those two months at The Compound were the first time I felt completely comfortable in my own skin. It's like up until that point in my life I'd been walking on a wire, trying to keep my balance. There, for the first time, I was on solid ground."

Though their relationship had shifted from contractual Master and slave to partners, Hailey was still a woman of few words most of the time. She was more of a listener, her intelligent eyes focused with complete attention on whoever was speaking. Ronan suspected this trait was partially a result of her yoga training, and partly a function of her naturally submissive nature. He understood from her uncharacteristic volubility just how excited his slave girl was to be returning to The Compound. Her excitement was contagious, and it felt good to be a part of it.

The door was opened by a burly, barrel-chested man with curly brown hair, naked save for black thong underwear and a black slave collar secured around his neck with a steel padlock. The man nodded with polite deference to Ronan. If he recognized him from the movies, he gave no indication, which suited Ronan just fine.

The man's face broke into a broad grin when his eyes lighted on Hailey, who exclaimed, "Sam! How are you? It's so good to see you." The two of them embraced.

Hailey turned to Ronan. "Master Ronan, this is Sam, a service slave here at The Compound, and witness to some of my most embarrassing moments."

"I have no idea what she's talking about," Sam said, his eyes dancing, and Ronan liked him at once. Sam pulled the door open wide and stepped back, gesturing them inside. "Mistress Miriam couldn't be here to greet you, Master Ronan, but she asked me to give you a quick tour and then show you to your cabin. Dinner is at seven o'clock so you have a little time to, uh, relax." He flashed another grin. "You'll find the guest cabin is fully equipped for *relaxing*."

Sam led them through a large, sumptuously furnished room, the walnut-paneled walls hung with gold-framed oil paintings. Ronan revised his initial impression of old farmhouse, upgrading it to English castle. "This is the drawing room," Sam said. "It's the hub of activity in the evenings." Waving toward the St. Andrew's crosses flanking either side of a huge stone fireplace, he added, "This is where presentations, demonstrations and ceremonies take place. There's something going on almost every night of the week." He looked at Hailey. "It wasn't that long ago this slave girl stood trembling over there during her first public flogging. Remember, Hailey?"

"Remember? How could I forget? My legs were so wobbly I would have fallen down if I hadn't been strapped to the cross. I much preferred kneeling with the other trainees against the wall, just taking it all in. I especially loved watching the ceremonies."

"You're in luck, girlfriend," Sam said. "Tonight slave Alexis is going to take Master Paul's ring in a piercing ceremony."

"Oh," Hailey exclaimed, drawing out the word with such obvious longing it made Ronan smile, while at the same time his cock nudged to attention. They'd talked about needle play and piercing before, and each time Hailey had demurely claimed it was up to him, but clearly the desire was there, along with the trepidation.

Sam led them up a wide, curving flight of stairs to the second floor. "Most of the trainers live on this floor," Sam explained, waving his hand toward a hallway of closed doors. "Those that aren't part of a couple, that is. The couples live out back in the cabins, where you'll be staying for the weekend."

He led them up a second flight of stairs, this one narrower. A large, fully equipped dungeon took up most of the third floor. Unlike the windowless cinderblock and cement basement dungeon to which Ronan had become accustomed at The Exchange back in LA, this place was more like something Hailey would have designed for a yoga studio. The space was filled with natural light from skylights overhead, the walls painted a peaceful pale blue.

There were easily a half dozen scenes going on at various locations around the large, open space, each involving some form of bondage and erotic torture. The slaves-in-training were all naked, save for red training collars around their necks. The male trainers wore black, most of them in T-shirts and casual pants or jeans, the one female trainer in an ankle-length black skirt.

Hailey's grip tightened suddenly on Ronan's hand. "Sir! Look over there. Is that George?" She craned her head forward. "It *is* George! What's he doing here?"

Ronan followed her gaze, breaking into a broad smile as he saw his old friend, who looked to be in fine form. George was dressed in full BDSM regalia, from his black leather vest and pants to his shiny black combat boots. He was standing next to a tall, broad-shouldered man with short blond hair. The man was using a single tail on a woman Ronan guessed to be somewhere in her fifties, though still lovely by anyone's estimation. She had silver hair, cut very short against a small, delicate head. Her pixyish figure was still trim and firm. She was perched on a large cinderblock, her bare feet close together as she balanced on the brick. Her arms were raised high over her head, bound together at the wrists and suspended from the ceiling by a length of chain.

As they moved closer, the trainer held out the whip in George's direction. As George turned to take it, he caught sight of them approaching. "Hey there. You made it. Welcome. Can't talk now. I'm busy." He turned back to the trainee, leaning close to murmur something in her ear. The young trainer had stepped back. Crossing his arms over his chest, he regarded the pair with round blue eyes, a frown of concentration on his serious face.

"You knew George would be here?" Hailey asked softly, looking up at Ronan with an inquisitive expression.

"Yeah." Ronan smiled. "A surprise for you. You mentioned the other day you missed him. He's been wanting to get back out to The Compound for reasons of his own, as you can see." Ronan looked pointedly at the handsome older woman, whose creamy skin was striped with small red welts. "He's been here already a few days. Miriam's call was perfect timing."

They stood quietly awhile, watching as George took over the session. He focused on the woman's breasts. While small, they had long, beautiful nipples, which were fully distended either from arousal, the kiss of the whip, or both. As George flicked the leather tail against her skin, he periodically touched her face or stroked her shoulder.

The woman did an admirable job of maintaining her composure and grace, but several particularly cruel strokes of the whip directly on her nipples made her cry out. She began to writhe in her bonds, chanting, "I can't! I can't! I can't!"

"Slave Sophia," barked the young trainer, "compose yourself!"

But George put a hand on the trainer's arm and shook his head. Lowering the whip, he leaned in close to Sophia. He cupped her cheek and murmured in a low, calm voice into her ear. She was trembling, but her cries subsided almost at once to a whimper, and then a sigh. The way she leaned into George's hand like a kitten, her large brown eyes fixed on his face, made Ronan wonder if these two were more than acquaintances.

Sam lightly touched Ronan's shoulder. "Shall I show you to your cabin, Sir?"

"What?" Ronan forced his eyes away from the scene. "Yes, of course, thank you."

They returned to the first floor, moving through a large, imposing dining room past a kitchen bustling with staff and out a back door. They walked along well-tended paths set between manicured lawns. As they walked, Sam pointed to the long single-story building Ronan had taken for horse stables upon their arrival. "That's the Slave Quarters," Sam said. "For the trainees."

"Did you stay there?" Ronan asked Hailey, who nodded. "Where do the staff slaves stay?" he asked Sam.

"We have rooms in the basement of the main house," Sam said.

"How many people live and work on this compound?" Ronan asked, curious. "Everything seems so well-kept and beautifully maintained."

"Let's see," Sam said, squinting up at the sky as he pondered. "We have two full-time chefs. One lives off-grounds, the other lives here. We have six full-time staff slaves and eight trainers, not counting Mistress Miriam. Two of the trainers don't actually live on the grounds. Three of the trainers are in relationships, and they stay out in the cabins. Mistress Miriam and her partner, slave Marta, have a bedroom on the first floor of the main house. There's a landscaping and housekeeping company that takes care of the grounds and that crew comes in daily."

A naked slave and his trainer passed them on the path at that moment, the slave being led by a leash. Watching them pass, Ronan asked, "How do you maintain privacy and protect peoples' confidentiality with all those outsiders coming and going?"

"Everyone involved in this place—from gardener to kitchen worker to our accountant, who also happens to be a staff slave—is into the scene, no exceptions," Sam explained. "On top of that, everyone signs strict confidentiality agreements to assure our lifestyle isn't compromised. Nothing we do here is illegal, but we do value our privacy, as you might imagine. Mistress Marta owns all the farmland around here, and we're left to ourselves. It's a safe haven—a paradise, really, for people seeking this kind of community."

Sam left them at a two-room cabin with a small galley kitchen. In addition to the usual bedroom and living room furniture, it also had its own St. Andrew's cross and a spanking bench. The bed was outfitted with leather restraints secured to the wrought iron frame of the four-poster bed. Several beautiful whips were artfully hung on the walls around the bedroom, whether for actual use or decoration, Ronan wasn't sure.

He sat on the bed, watching his slave girl tuck their few belongings into bureau drawers. "Slave Hailey," Ronan said, "come over here."

She immediately stopped what she was doing and came to stand in front of him. She was wearing a pale pink sleeveless blouse tucked into a black skirt. He'd allowed bra and underwear for the drive from Vermont to New York, but had a sudden, urgent need to see her naked.

"Slave girls, even visiting ones, should be naked while staying at The Compound, don't you agree?"

"Yes, Sir," she said softly, lowering her eyes so her long lashes brushed her soft cheeks. The whole atmosphere of the place was drenched in eroticism and sensuality, and this beautiful, submissive woman standing before him only stoked the flames lit by watching the scenes in the dungeon. They had about an hour before dinner, but it wouldn't have mattered what time it was, or what appointments were waiting, he had to have her *now*.

Hailey had already unbuttoned several of the buttons on her blouse, but Ronan couldn't wait another second. He reached for the blouse, ripping it open in a spray of buttons. Grabbing her, he pulled her down onto the bed and pushed her skirt up to her waist. Hooking his fingers beneath the elastic of her panties, he yanked them down and tossed them aside.

Hailey was panting as she reached for his jeans and tugged at the metal buttons of his fly. Lifting himself over her, he pushed his pants and underwear down his legs, too eager even to bother kicking them away.

He was nearly shaking with need as he positioned the head of his cock at her opening. Knees spread wide, Hailey lifted her hips, at the same time grabbing his hips and pulling him down onto and into her. "Please, Sir," she begged breathily. "Fuck me. Use me. Claim me."

She was wet with desire, her cunt sucking him in and catching his shaft in a tight, hot clutch of pleasure. They thrashed on the bed, grunting and growling with animal lust. Though a pleasant breeze blew through the open bedroom window, sweat slicked between them as Ronan swiveled and thrust inside her. Within minutes, Hailey began to tremble. She clutched at his back, her nails grazing his skin. "Please, oh god, oh god, oh please—" Her words were cut short by a gasp and a long, low moan. She had come before he could even get out the words to grant permission.

Ronan pulled from her spasming cunt and flipped her roughly onto her stomach. Grabbing her hips, he jerked her ass upward. He would have liked to ram himself into her tight ass, but he didn't have the time or inclination to find the tube of lubricant, and wasn't so crazed with lust to forget his responsibility as her Dom never to harm her. So instead he pushed again into her tight, wet cunt, his fingers digging into her hips as he eased her onto his shaft.

Within seconds, his balls tightened and he felt the shuddering pulse of a powerful climax rip its way through his body. He wrapped his arms around Hailey's body, pulling her close against him until his spasms subsided. He collapsed onto the bed, taking Hailey with him as he fell. He rolled onto his back, still holding her in his arms. She curled tightly against his side and rubbed his chest with her cheek, her hair a golden sprawl obscuring her face.

He stroked her back as they rested. "You were a very bad girl, slave Hailey," he murmured eventually, smiling over her head though he tried to keep his voice stern. "What happens to naughty slave girls who come without permission?"

She stiffened against him and he almost felt sorry for her, though he knew she craved and needed the punishments that were part and parcel of their D/s relationship. "They are punished, Sir. I'm sorry, Sir."

"That's right, slave girl. Rest assured you will be punished."

Hailey said nothing, but a small tremor moved through her slim form. Ronan held her closer and kissed the top of her head. The comfortable bed, the cool breeze fluttering the curtains, the aftermath of a powerful orgasm, all combined to pull him toward sleep. "I love you," he murmured, staying awake only long enough to hear her like reply.

~*~

It was fantastic to be back at The Compound, but even more amazing to be there with Master Ronan. She was no longer a slave in training, yearning for connection. She was kneeling on her cushion beside *her* Master at the long dining room table. George was on Ronan's left, with Hailey between them, Sophia on a cushion on his other side. Hailey recognized most of the faces of the people sitting around the table, and many of the slaves and subs kneeling serenely beside them.

Mistress Miriam presided at the head of the table as always, striking with her dark hair and blue eyes. She wore a tailored midnight blue silk jacket over toffee-colored leather pants. Marta, her partner, knelt quietly beside her Mistress, leaning with closed eyes against Mistress Miriam's hand as she absently stroked Marta's cheek while talking to Ronan.

Hailey couldn't wait to talk to Alexis, who knelt beside her partner, Master Paul, a handsome man with long auburn hair and tawny, coppery eyes. Master John, who had been working with George in the dungeon, sat across the table, his adoring slave girl Wendy at his side.

The main course had been served, and staff was clearing and preparing for dessert and coffee. While Ronan was engaged with Mistress Miriam, George looked down at Hailey. "I missed you, little girl," he said, smiling fondly at her. "I missed Ronan too." They exchanged a few minutes of small talk, and then George surprised Hailey by saying, "I'm not just here at The Compound for a visit. After you guys left, I really got to thinking about what my own priorities are. I'm a widower, you know, and I'm definitely not getting any younger. I was pretty involved at the BDSM club where I met Ronan, but that kind of place can only take you so far. Watching you and Ronan together made me realize I wanted something like that in my life, too. After you two disappeared, I decided to take the plunge. My condo is on the market, and I've signed up here at The Compound. I'm officially a trainer in training," he said with a proud grin. "Who knows?" he glanced down at Sophia. "Maybe someday I'll even claim a girl of my own."

After dinner, Hailey had an opportunity to reconnect with Alexis. Alexis was beautiful by all accounts, with smooth olive skin, long dark hair and large, expressive brown eyes. Her breasts were heavy and full, the dark nipples beautifully set off by gold hoops, which hadn't been there the last time Hailey had seen her.

"Wow," Hailey said enviously. "That jewelry is gorgeous. Did it hurt?"

"Like a motherfucker," Alexis assented with a grin. "But totally worth it. I love them!"

"So the piercing tonight..." Hailey prompted.

Alexis placed a hand over her smooth mons. "Lower down," she said.

"Are you nervous?"

"What do you think? Of course I am. But I want it. I've been thinking of nothing else for the past month since we first started talking about it."

Hailey nodded, well understanding that delicious dichotomy of fear and desire so common in the submissive experience.

"Hey!" Alexis said suddenly, reaching for Hailey's left hand. She pointed to the large, square-cut diamond flanked by a dark blue sapphire on either side. "Is that what I think it is? Are you engaged?"

Hailey flushed with pleasure. "I am," she agreed. "Though we haven't set an official date yet." She looked down at her beautiful ring, her heart full of happiness. "Probably sometime next spring."

"I'm so happy for you," Alexis said with feeling. Hailey glanced sharply at her, sensing the yearning in her words and seeing the longing in her face. Alexis had come to The Compound for training the year before Hailey, and had ended up falling in love with one of the trainers. She'd happily left behind her life as a Manhattan CPA to make her home at The

Compound, and when she wasn't handling the facility's financial books, she worked in tandem with Master Paul to train new submissives. She had told Hailey marriage wasn't in the cards for Master Paul and her—they were Master and slave, and it was all they needed. Hailey had believed her at the time, but now she wondered.

There was the sound of masculine laughter, and they looked over to see Master Paul and Master Ronan talking. It pleased Hailey to think they might become friends. "You know, your guy is a dead ringer for that action hero dude. What's his name, Ronan Wolfe? Except he's even better looking than the guy on the screen."

Hailey laughed. "I didn't realize I'd never told you his name! Actually, he *is* that action hero dude. Or was. He's retired from acting."

Alexis' eyes grew round. "He *is* Ronan Wolfe? Oh my god! That's insane! Do you live in some Beverly Hills mansion surrounded by bodyguards?"

Hailey shook her head. "No. He was living in Malibu when he first bought my contract. He was pretty miserable, really. He never liked all the publicity and harassment that goes along with the whole movie star fame thing. Then, when the mystery girl video went viral, we decided just to get out of town for a while. He's made the decision that he doesn't ever want to go back to that kind of life, or that career, which is fine with me. He went from living in a huge, sprawling mansion in California to my little cottage in a small Vermont town, but he's happier than I've ever seen him."

Alexis furrowed her brown. "Wait. Back it up a second. Mystery girl video? What's that?"

Hailey realized Alexis was actually asking—she really didn't know. What a relief to realize the entire planet wasn't connected to the daily gossip rife on the internet. "Never mind," she said quickly. "I'll tell you later."

"Okay. But I want a full report."

Master Paul and Master Ronan approached at that moment. "Paul and I were just discussing a few things we have in common." They exchanged a quick glance, their smiles conspiratorial. Ronan continued, "Among the things we addressed is the matter of your punishment, slave Hailey," Ronan said, his words sending a shiver through Hailey's loins. She reached up to stroke the soft leather of her slave collar as he continued. "Master Paul agrees it would be fitting for you to be publically punished prior to the piercing ceremony this evening. You'll be the opening act, if you will."

He wasn't asking her for her input or permission. Though a thousand butterflies were now flapping giddily inside her, Hailey replied as calmly as she could manage, "Yes, Sir. Thank you, Sir."

At nine o'clock the drawing room was packed with people eager to witness Alexis' piercing. There were six women and one man kneeling at attention against the wall, naked bodies proudly displayed, eyes properly downcast as they waited for the ceremony to begin. One of them was Sophia, the silver-haired beauty George had been working with that afternoon, and Hailey admired her courage at taking this step later in life. It wasn't that long ago that Hailey had been kneeling against that wall, eager to learn, terrified she might not have what it took to become a proper submissive. She sent each trainee a silent prayer of success and happiness.

Master Paul was sitting on a love seat near the fireplace, Alexis kneeling on a cushion on the carpet beside him with her head resting on his lap. A small table was set up beside the hearth, a piercing kit and a wooden jewelry box on its surface. There was also, oddly, a kitchen timer.

Mistress Miriam took center stage on the hearth and the room quieted. "As you know, tonight Master Paul will further claim his slave girl, Alexis, in a ritual piercing ceremony. But before that, we have a welcome guest here with us tonight, Master Ronan, as well as a graduate from the training program who most of you will remember, slave Hailey."

There was scattered applause and a few calls of welcome as Ronan led Hailey to the front of the room. "Unfortunately," Mistress Miriam continued in her lilting voice, "this slave girl was disobedient this afternoon, and her Master has chosen a public forum for her correction."

She turned her cool gaze on Hailey. "Tell the group, slave Hailey, what you did that led to this punishment."

Hailey gazed in mute appeal at her Master, but knew there was no way out. At The Compound, Mistress Miriam reigned supreme. Hailey's legs felt rubbery and her face was burning with embarrassment. She drew in a deep, shuddering breath and closed her eyes, calling on her mantra to calm herself: *Serenity. Peace. Submission. Grace.* Ronan placed his hand on the small of her back, and his touch, even more than her mantra, centered her.

She opened her eyes and faced her friends. "I sometimes have trouble controlling my orgasm. This afternoon I didn't manage to get permission in time." There was some laughter, all of it kind, and nods of sympathetic understanding from other subs in the room.

"Mistress Miriam and I agreed," Master Ronan said, stepping away from Hailey and reaching for a sturdy wooden chair, "that, given slave Hailey's lack of discipline, we'd use tonight's punishment as a kind of practice session. We're going to bind the slave to the chair. I'm going to invite five volunteers to come up and stimulate her for three minutes each." He turned to face Hailey. "Your punishment, slave girl, is to exhibit self-control. You will *not* ask for permission to orgasm, and you *will not* come. Are we crystal clear on this?"

Hailey swallowed at the sudden lump that had risen in her throat. "Yes, Sir," she managed to croak. Master Paul joined them on the hearth. Hailey was instructed to sit on the chair, ass perched on the front edge of the seat. Her ankles were bound to the legs of the chair, her wrists cuffed behind her. She was thankful at least she'd been permitted to sit, and she promised herself to resist climax at all costs.

Sam was the first volunteer. The timer was started, and he knelt between Hailey's legs, his thick fingers pushing her thighs apart as he ducked his head to lick and tease her sex. Hailey understood at that moment how far she had come in terms of acceptance and comfort in allowing others to give her pleasure.

A skilled service slave, Sam knew exactly when to apply pressure and when to pull back, and it wasn't long before Hailey found her defenses rapidly weakening. She forced her eyes, which had somehow fluttered closed, to open, and she focused on the stern Master John, who was regarding her with his unblinking, owl-like stare, his lips pursed in anticipatory disapproval.

It worked, and Hailey managed to resist Sam's onslaught until the timer dinged. He leaned back and wiped his mouth with his hand, offering her a surreptitious thumbs-up as he rose to his feet. The second volunteer was Marta, who took her position behind Hailey. Leaning over her so their cheeks touched, she massaged Hailey's spread cunt with her fingers, rubbing her palm against Hailey's clit as she pressed the digits inside.

Hailey bit her lip, sweat beading on her forehead and under her arms as she struggled to resist Marta's spot-on manipulations. Master John was now positively glowering, and Hailey shifted her gaze to the slaves in training, all of whom were watching her, several of them with their mouths agape. She would resist for them. She would be strong for them all.

The timer dinged. Marta withdrew her hand. "Good job," she whispered as she stepped back. "Stay strong."

Two more volunteers took their turns between her legs and somehow, miraculously, she resisted the nearly overpowering urge to succumb to their touch. The fifth volunteer, to her surprise, was Master Ronan. With an evil grin, he took his place, dipping his head to cover her mons and labia with dozens of tiny, electrifying kisses. She knew this would be her hardest test yet. She tried to look at the forbidding Master John to get her bearings, but she couldn't manage to focus. Ronan's kisses were those not only of a Master, but of a lover intimately familiar with every curve and sweet spot.

Hailey forced her eyes open. She bit down hard on her lower lip and pressed her fingernails into her palms, hoping the pain would distract her enough to stay strong. She twisted in an effort to see the timer, which tick-tick-ticked the seconds away. *Two minutes left. You can do this. You do it. Focus. Think about bugs and vomit and assholes from high school. Resist. Resist. Resist.* She bit down harder and tasted the metallic trickle of blood. The timer dinged. Master Ronan lifted his head, but instead of rising to his feet, he said in a low, sensual voice, "The punishment is over. Now come for me, slave Hailey. You have my permission."

He ducked his head again and lapped eagerly at her clit while slipping a single, wet fingertip into her ass. Hailey didn't need to be told twice. She came as hard as she ever had, shuddering and bucking in her bonds, her heart thudding in her ears, her breath rasping in her throat as a tsunami of pleasure momentarily obliterated all conscious thought.

The room erupted in thunderous applause and laughter, and Hailey, while embarrassed, basked in the glow of such total acceptance and love. The ropes were quickly untied, and Master Ronan scooped Hailey into his arms, carrying her to the love seat that had been vacated by Alexis and Master Paul, who now stood side-by-side by the hearth.

Hailey expected Master Ronan to set her on the silk cushion at his feet, but he kept her in his arms as he sat, and she certainly didn't protest. As she snuggled against him, her focus returned to the front of the room, where Alexis was now being prepared for her piercing.

A reclining bondage chair was brought to the center of the hearth, and Alexis was strapped into it, her legs spread wide. With assistance from Master Clarence, who was an expert in piercing and branding, Alexis' clit hood was prepped for piercing. Master Paul turned to face the audience. "My slave girl has asked for another piercing, this one on her clit hood, as a constant reminder of her servitude, love and devotion. We are honored to share this ceremony with our community tonight."

There were murmurs, nods and smiles. Master Paul turned to Alexis, the piercing needle in his hand. "Slave Alexis," he said in a loud voice, though his eyes were fixed solely on her face, "do you willingly accept this gift as further testament of our unbreakable bond as Master and slave?"

"Yes, Sir," Alexis said, her face soft with love.

The room was utterly silent as, under Clarence's watchful eye, Master Paul slipped the piercing needle through the delicate membrane. Other than a small, sudden gasp, Alexis remained still and quiet, though her hands had clenched into fists. Clarence handed Paul the ring, which he threaded quickly into place.

He stepped back, announcing, "It is done," and again the room burst into applause. The two men released Alexis' restraints and helped her to her feet. Hailey expected Master Paul to lead his girl to a sofa, or for them to leave the room to recover together in the privacy of their cabin.

Ronan shifted and Hailey glanced at him, surprised to see he was grinning like a cat that ate the canary, his gaze fixed expectantly on Master Paul. What was going on?

Hailey followed his gaze and was shocked to see Master Paul drop to one knee. Alexis seemed shocked as well, or at the very least completely surprised by his action. Master Paul held out his hand. Hailey could see the glitter of gold and diamond against his open palm. The room once again stilled to absolute silence. "This ring is for you as well," he said, smiling up at her, "though this one won't require another piercing." In a louder voice, he continued, "Alexis, my slave girl, my darling, the light of my life. Will you accept this ring as a symbol of the never-ending circle of our love? Will you marry me?"

Alexis' hands flew to her mouth, tears filling her pretty dark eyes. She dropped to her knees and reached for Paul, catching him in a tight embrace. "Yes!" she cried, and Hailey couldn't tell if she was laughing or crying, and decided she was doing both. "Yes, my Master, my love, I will marry you."

Amidst the cheering and clapping, Hailey turned to Ronan. "You knew, didn't you! That's what all that was about before—you were in on this!"

"Guilty as charged," Ronan admitted with a devilish grin. "What would you think about a double wedding here at The Compound? I'm thinking you'd look lovely in white lace and a few piercings of your own. Sound good?"

Hailey laughed, pulling Ronan's head down for a kiss. "Yes," she agreed. "Sounds perfect."

Chapter 13

They'd been home a few days and were lingering over their second cups of coffee when Hailey said, "Excuse me, Sir, but may I speak?"

Since they'd become engaged, the "rules" as such, had changed, and Ronan no longer required his slave girl to ask permission to speak. However, she'd maintained the formality when she wished to ask something directly to do with BDSM, especially when it was something she was uncomfortable or shy about approaching. Ronan understood her need for the comfort of ritual in those instances, and so replied, "Yes, slave Hailey. What is it?"

"Well" — her cheeks turned a little pink and her hand moved to fondle her collar — "remember at the piercing ceremony, what you said about us — I mean about me? About piercings and lace?"

In the months they'd been together, Hailey had exhibited a love-hate relationship with the idea of piercing. She appreciated the symbolism and esthetic beauty of the jewelry, but remained frightened of needles. They had discussed her continued resistance as something they would work on overcoming together, but so far she hadn't been ready, and it wasn't something he would force on her — it had to be freely given or not at all.

"I remember," he said, keeping his tone casual. "What about it?"

Her cheeks got even pinker, and Ronan resisted the urge to smile at her fluster. "I was thinking," she began, "um…" He waited. She took a breath and then plunged forward, the words tumbling over one another. "I want it. I want my nipples pierced, Sir. I want it done before the wedding ceremony so they have time to heal. I want to wear your piercings, Sir, as symbols of your ownership over my body and heart."

"I would like that very much," Ronan replied gravely. "I've been waiting for this day, sweet slave. I just happen to have a piercing kit and some jewelry all picked out. I've been keeping it for when you were ready."

Hailey's eyes widened in surprise and pleasure. "Really?"

Ronan nodded, smiling. "Really and truly. I had several lessons with Clarence and I feel confident I can do this for you. Or, if you'd rather, we can go to The Compound and have it done there."

Hailey jumped up from the table and threw her arms around Ronan's neck. "You're the best Master in the world!" she cried with uncharacteristic abandon. "Thank you, Sir. I promise to be brave and strong. Let's do it today, okay? Let's do it now!"

Ronan laughed and gently disengaged from Hailey's enthusiastic embrace. "Don't you have two classes to teach this morning? I'm not sure you'd want to go directly from a piercing to the yoga studio."

"Oh, yeah. Damn," Hailey muttered, furrowing her brows. Then she brightened. "I could cancel them, or reschedule. I could — "

"No." Ronan shook his head. "You have responsibilities. You teach the classes, and I'll prepare for the piercing. The yoga classes should help you center yourself in anticipation of the piercing. We'll do it when you come home this afternoon."

The agitation ebbed from Hailey's countenance, serenity once again claiming her pretty face. "Yes, Sir. Thank you, Sir."

~*~

Summer was ending, but the day was still warm enough to allow Hailey to lie naked on the quilt beside the creek, save for her slave collar, which she only removed to shower. Ronan was crouched beside her, assembling the piercing kit items on a tray. The rings he'd chosen were as beautiful as the engagement ring he'd placed on her finger. Made of white gold, the beads that held the jewelry in place were inlaid with tiny diamonds shaped into the petals of a flower. Rather than the large, sharp needles, gauze, gloves and clamps that also lay in waiting on the tray, Hailey chose to focus only on the delicate, exquisite jewelry.

Ever since Alexis' piercing ceremony, Hailey had been more determined than ever to finally move past her fear of needles. In some ways she had been waiting and hoping Master Ronan would make the decision for her, and simply inform her that she would be pierced, but she understood enough now about the nature of their D/s bond to recognize he would never push something on her she wasn't fully prepared to give.

Ronan gently cleaned her nipples with a sterile solution, which he also used on the clamps that would hold each nipple taut while he inserted the threading needle. Hailey closed her eyes at this point, keeping the image of the sparkling jewelry in her mind's eye as she silently chanted her serenity mantra.

"We'll do the right nipple first," Master Ronan said. She felt the tug of the surgical clamps closing on her nipple. She drew in a deep breath and released it slowly, letting the lulling sound of the creek water rushing over stones calm her. "You will feel a burning, pinching sensation. Hold very still, and it will be over quickly."

"Yes, Sir," she breathed, pleased her voice came out calmer than she felt. Her heart was hammering in her chest, and she drew in another cleansing breath.

"At the count of three, I'll thread the needle through and then the jewelry." Hailey nodded, though she kept her eyes closed. "One…two…three."

The pain was sudden and sharp, like a hot poker shoving its way through her flesh. In spite of her promise to herself to remain quiet, Hailey yelped.

"Done!" Ronan said triumphantly.

Hailey felt woozy and knew if she hadn't been lying down, she would have probably passed out. As it was, she just lay there, inert, eyes closed. A strange sense of elation was swirling through her, displacing the fear and the lingering throb of pain at the piercing site.

"Second one will be even easier," Ronan said soothingly. "Just hold still a moment longer. You're doing great." She felt the tug of the clamps at her left nipple and then the cold prick of the needle, which morphed into a sudden, pinching fire.

And then it was done.

She opened her eyes. Ronan was grinning down at her. "You did it! You were perfect. I'm so proud of you. Want to see?"

Hailey started to lift herself and Ronan reached quickly behind her, helping her to a sitting position. He picked up the hand mirror from the tray and held it so she could see. Hailey stared down at the image in awe. Her nipples were engorged and dark red, and she knew they would be tender for a few days, but the jewelry was beautiful, the diamond flowers winking in the sunlight that dappled through the maples overhead.

Joy and pride bubbled up through her, erupting into a startled laugh. "I did it! I mean, you did it."

"*We* did it," Ronan agreed with a laugh.

~*~

It was as if the leaves on the trees had been advised of the upcoming ceremony. Almost overnight they had changed into their fall finery, brilliant yellows, reds and oranges festooning the branches and falling in soft, sudden showers to the ground. While there was a slight chill in the air, all agreed the double wedding ceremony would still take place outside as planned.

Hailey and Ronan had decided to have a simple ceremony later in the month for their vanilla relations, and just leave out the little detail that they would already be married. Alexis and Paul, too, had made alternate arrangements for their non-BDSM counterparts.

The four of them lolled on a blanket by the old barn near Alexis and Paul's cabin after lunch. Alexis was snuggled beside Paul. Ronan rested against the trunk of a shade tree, Hailey leaning back against his chest. As he looked over at his new friends, Ronan understood on a gut level that The Compound was more than just a highly specialized slave training facility, and even more than a close-knit BDSM community. It was a safe and soul-nurturing place that provided the kindred connection that truly defined family.

Later that afternoon, when the girls were off together trying on their wedding outfits and doing whatever girls did to get ready for such events,

Ronan, Paul and George sat out by the pool behind the main house.

"So, it's official, huh? That's great!" Ronan said.

"Yep." George grinned happily. "I signed the papers with Miriam this morning. I'm going to be a full-time trainer." He shook his head, a look of wonder moving over his craggy face. "You know, when I was here last year scoping out the place for you, I remember thinking how fantastic it would be to live here, but it never occurred to me it might actually happen someday. I'm no spring chicken, you know. I just turned sixty-three, for god's sake. I've been a widower for seven years. I've been retired for three. Who ever thought I'd be starting a whole new career at this point in my life?"

Paul laughed. "Are you kidding? Sixty is the new forty, haven't you heard?"

"Hell," Ronan interjected. "In LA it's the new twenty-five, with the right plastic surgeon." They all laughed.

"But you left something out in that little summation of your new life, didn't you, George?" Paul added, his eyes twinkling. "Or rather, someone?"

George did something Ronan had never seen before. He blushed.

"What?" Ronan demanded, and then he knew. "Sophia! Isn't she about done with her training at this point?"

George nodded. "She was working with Master John when I first started observing and working with him. We really hit it off, and she's going to stay on at The Compound as a kitchen staff slave. She's a terrific dessert chef, so we're all going to get fat!" He laughed, patting his stomach, which was still flat and firm, despite his age.

"Okay, he's not going to come out and say it, so I will," Paul said, turning to Ronan. "The two of them are as head over heels in love as teenagers. George didn't want to upstage our double wedding, so they're waiting until next month to have their own claiming ceremony. George is going to take Sophia as his slave, and they'll move out to one of the cabins."

Ronan stood to embrace his old friend. "I'm so happy for you, George. Maybe we should do a triple wedding—why not?"

George chuckled. "Nah. Soph and I don't go in for that establishment bullshit. We're children of the sixties, don't forget. We'd way rather live in sin."

~*~

They stood beneath a large wedding canopy, which from a distance looked like any other, festooned with flowers and vines. But on closer inspection, the dangling chains, rope and leather wound among the foliage added a festive BDSM touch. Hailey and Alexis were both dressed in sheer lace dresses that had been specially tailored for them by a BDSM wedding designer friend of Alexis' from

New York City. They were both naked beneath the gowns, save for their respective piercings. Ronan and Paul looked dashing in black leather pants and white silk shirts.

Mistress Miriam presided over the ceremony, which was brief but very romantic. The couples had written out their vows beforehand, and the four of them took turns reading them to their respective partners. It was a good thing she had her index card with the vows neatly typed out, because Hailey was in such a daze of nerves and excitement that she barely remembered her own name, much less the pretty words they'd spent the past month composing for this special day.

They moved inside after the ceremony. The drawing room had been rearranged to make space for dancing. Everyone had been invited to the party, and the room was filled with staff and trainees, the subs in the group easily identifiable by their lack of clothing, which lent a sensual, erotic air to the festivities.

The cake, a seven-tiered masterpiece of coconut and buttercream prepared by Sophia, was cut and served, and champagne corks popped all around the room. The music piped through the sound system was smoky jazz, perfect for slow dancing, and it wasn't long before the dance floor was filled with swaying couples. The usually stern Master John was looking down at his slave girl, Wendy, with such tenderness it made Hailey's heart catch in her throat. George held Sophia in his arms, and they had eyes only for each other. Mistress Miriam and Marta were quite accomplished dancers, doing some kind of complicated moves that reminded Hailey of the old Fred Astaire and Ginger Rogers movies, a small, appreciative crowd gathering around them in admiration.

Sam, Hailey noticed between dance numbers, when Ronan had left her a moment to get them each a piece of cake, was sitting alone near the fireplace, his expression contemplative, even sad. Hailey moved toward him, and he looked up with a quick smile. "Hey there, Mrs. Wolfe," he said. "The ceremony was beautiful."

Hailey smiled back. "It was, wasn't it?" She sat beside him, her smile falling away. Sam, dear Sam, steadfast and kind, never judgmental even in the face of the trainees' worst disgraces, had always seemed to Hailey a haven of calm acceptance — the very essence of a serene service slave. It honestly hadn't occurred to her he might have troubles of his own.

"Excuse me if I'm intruding," she ventured, "but you looked so sad just now, Sam. Is everything okay?"

Sam shrugged. "Sure, everything's fine. It's just..." He paused, the sad, faraway look again coming into his eyes. "I miss him sometimes."

"Who?"

"Jamie. My partner. We were together a long time. He passed away—gosh, it's been five years now. He had cancer. It was a blessing in the end, really." He flashed another smile, though there were tears in his eyes. Hailey put her hand over his, her heart aching for her friend. "I'm fine, really," he asserted. "I made my peace with it a long time ago. It's just at times like this..."

"I understand. I do," Hailey said. "I'm glad you have this wonderful community. But I know it can be lonely. Before I met Master Ronan, I honestly didn't know if I would ever find a man I could connect with on every level." She squeezed his hand. "You're still young. You never know who's going to come into your life, Sam."

Sam shook his head. "Nah. I'm done with that. I had my true love." He smiled again, this time with conviction. "I have a fantastic life here at The Compound. I have friends and community, and work that fulfills me. I love being a service slave."

Hailey nodded. "That's wonderful, Sam. All I would say is, remain open. Don't shut yourself down to the possibility of something new."

"Excuse me, I don't mean to interrupt. We haven't met yet, but I wanted to congratulate you, Hailey. The ceremony was beautiful."

Hailey looked up to see a tall man with dark hair and a large, hawkish nose in a long, narrow face. He was handsome in a craggy cowboy kind of way. He wore dark jeans and a black leather vest over a lean but muscular frame.

Sam jumped to his feet, looking suddenly flustered. "Master Andrew. Allow me to present slave Hailey. She trained here at The Compound." He turned to Hailey, spots of color on his cheeks. He was acting, Hailey suddenly thought, like a teenager with a crush. "Hailey, Master Andrew just signed up last week. He's an expert in whip handling and fire play. We're really lucky to get him."

Master Andrew held out his hand, and Hailey shook it. "A pleasure to meet you. I look forward to knowing you and Master Ronan better." He dropped her hand and stepped back. "The music is perfect for dancing," he began, and Hailey, whose feet were aching in the unaccustomed heels she was wearing, wondered if she could gracefully decline.

But Master Andrew had turned to Sam. "Slave Sam, would you like to dance?"

"I-I would be honored, Sir," Sam stammered sweetly, taking the man's proffered hand. As he followed Master Andrew to the dance floor, he turned back to Hailey with a broad grin and a shrug.

Ronan appeared at Hailey's side, balancing two glasses of champagne and two plates of cake in his hands. "Are you happy, sweetheart?" he said, as he handed her a plate and glass.

"Very," she said smiling. "There's love in the air tonight, Ronan, and not just ours." She looked toward the dance floor, where Sam was now enfolded in Master Andrew's arms. They were talking as they danced. Master Andrew said something, and Sam laughed.

Ronan followed her gaze and grinned. He lifted his champagne toward the dance floor. "To new beginnings," he said.

"To us," she replied, lifting her glass to clink it against his. "All of us here at The Compound, and beyond."

Available at Romance Unbound Publishing

(http://romanceunbound.com)

Jewel Thief
Julie's Submission
Lara's Submission
Masked Submission
Obsession: Girl Abducted
Odd Man Out
Pleasure Planet
Princess
Safe in His Arms
Sarah's Awakening
Seduction of Colette
Slave Academy
Slave Castle
Slave Gamble
Slave Girl
Slave Island
Slave Jade
Sold into Slavery
Stardust
Sub for Hire
Submission in Paradise
Submission Times Two
Switch
Switching Gears
Texas Surrender
The Auction
The Compound
The Contract
The Cowboy Poet
The Inner Room

Connect with Claire

Website: http://clairethompson.net
Romance Unbound Publishing:
http://romanceunbound.com
Twitter: http://twitter.com/CThompsonAuthor
Facebook:
http://www.facebook.com/ClaireThompsonauthor
Blog: http://clairethompsonauthor.blogspot.com

Made in the USA
Charleston, SC
03 October 2015